FETISH DREAMS

The Purgatory Collection

Books by Eliza Gayle

SUBMISSIVE BEAUTY
TUCKER'S FALL
BOTTOM'S UP
MIDNIGHT PLAYGROUND
POWER PLAY
SWEET SUBMISSION
WICKED CHRISTMAS EVE
SUBMISSIVE SECRETS
HER SURRENDER

And don't miss these paranormal gems from
Eliza Gayle!

LUCAS
KANE
MALCOLM
THE BILLIONAIRE'S DEMON
FROST BITTEN
VAMPIRE AWAKENING
THEIR OBSESSION
UNTAMED MAGICK
MAGICK IGNIRED
FORCE OF MAGICK
MAGICK PROVOKED
BLACK MOON RISING
SLAVE TO PLEASURE

Fetish Dreams

The Purgatory Collection

Eliza Gayle

www.elizagayle.net

Fetish Dreams
The Purgatory Collection
Copyright © 2011 by Eliza Gayle
Cover art by: Kendra Egert

Gypsy Ink Books
www.gypsyinkbooks.wordpress.com

Dedication

To my family and friends who brighten my day with a few words of encouragement or the forgiveness they offer when I spend my days and nights tucked in my writing cave working on the stories I love.

Acknowledgments

You probably don't need me to tell you that BDSM play can be dangerous. However, even after extensive research, observations and direct information, mistakes do happen. This is a work of fiction and should be treated as such. Any mistakes in regards to the safety of BDSM play are my own. Before engaging in edge play such as fire, please consult a professional. Fire, when done right, is a wonder to behold.

Contents

Enjoy the first four Purgatory stories in this collector's edition.

Roped

Katie has a fetish for rope and she's had her eye on riggers Leo and Quinn for quite some time. Now the two hunky men have decided to make their move. But is plus-sized Katie ready to turn her fantasies into reality?

Displayed

For too long Emerson tried to gain the attention of one man, with no luck. Until she discovers his secret--in a sex club. Rio wants what he can't have but isn't about to ruin his life over it. Now a new woman has caught his eye and he longs to discover why she hides. As they get closer to the truth, the tension escalates and the forbidden becomes irresistible.

Whipped

Walker comes to Purgatory looking for a place to call home and a submissive for the long term. The second he lays eyes on Cass, his mind is made up. Cass enjoys the anonymity Purgatory gives her, as well as the freedom to live by her rules. Can Cass overcome her personal demons to give in completely to the Dom who has her heart, and a mighty strong whip, in his hands?

Burned

As a member of the staff, Ruby can experiment with her fire fetish without worrying about going too far or too deep into a scene she is certain she doesn't belong in. But there's one Dom in town who makes her burn for things she wishes she didn't. Zane kept his distance as long as he could but tonight he'll take possession of the willful beauty who has captured his heart.

Stay tuned after *Burned* for a sneak peek into the first Purgatory Masters book, Tucker's Fall!

ROPED

Katie watched Leo's hands stroke the woman's inner thigh with the rope as he tied it around her leg. She imagined the course texture scraping against her own sensitive skin, sending a shiver snaking along her spine. She continued to observe the twists and turns of the rope as they wrapped it around both her legs and waist. The girl giggled through the process but the lines etched in Leo's face showed just how serious he took his job. The loud beat of industrial music playing in the club pounded with her own heartbeat, pulsating through her body. Bodies crushed around her as the night's play got into full swing, but her attention remained solely on the rope.

She tuned it all out to focus on the station below. Soon both Leo and Quinn would hook the woman up to the swing and fling her across the club, but first he tied her. Wetness pooled between her thighs with the familiar longing to be the girl in Leo's hands, slowly tied from limb to limb until her freedom was stripped and her trust tested.

"Isn't it about time you quit watching and started feeling, Katie?" The familiar timber of Quinn's voice whispered in her ear as his arms grabbed the railing on either side of her, trapping her in his embrace. Her pulse skipped as she sucked in a shallow breath of surprise. "That could be you down there, feeling the rope across your belly, wrapped around your wrists and totally at his mercy."

Her nipples peaked against her shirt at the mere image his words brought to mind. She screwed her eyes closed tight, as she tried to stop the effect he was having on her.

"Shouldn't you be down there helping out your partner?" She tried to concentrate on her breathing but the man pressed against her back made her heart race and her body burn with renewed need. The heat alone was enough to make her weak in the knees.

"Come with me, Katie. Let me tie you."

She shook her head as fear gripped her body. She wasn't ready. She wasn't sure she could recover from either Leo or Quinn teasing her body like that.

Quinn grasped her wrist and flipped her around to face him. His amber eyes pierced through her with a heated intensity as he watched her reactions. "You come here week after week and stand here looking down at us as we work. Do you think we don't notice the longing on your face? The way your body squirms as we wrap more and more rope around the girls who ask us to? Why are you torturing yourself? Or should I say...what are you waiting for?"

She closed her eyes to his questions, searching for an adequate answer when she knew there was none. How could she deny the truth? "I admire your work. What's wrong with that?"

His fingers gently grasped her chin and tilted her head back, forcing her to look at him. "We see you, Katie, we know what you need. Why do you hide here?"

She bristled against his words, shame heating her face. "I'm not hiding, Quinn, I'm just observing. I'm here and I'm alone, yet no one ever approaches or speaks to me. Which is fine, but don't tell me that I'm hiding. What am I supposed to do? Throw myself at someone?"

A grin split Quinn's handsome face, revealing the beautiful smile she loved so much. She always noticed how happy his job made him and she envied him that feeling. Some ties were more intense than others as evidenced by the hard lines of his face when he concentrated or the occasional bulge in his pants when a willing female turned him on. It was those moments when she had fleeting thoughts of both him and Leo taking her for their own. The popular riggers were frequently gossiped about around Purgatory, and word was they had a great time playing the scene together but hadn't taken a submissive of their own for a very long time.

"You don't have to get defensive with me, babe. I'm not sure what's wrong with the men in this club, letting you spend all your time alone. Their loss is my gain, though." He leaned closer, his lips a breath away from her own. The sharp tang of citrus filled her nostrils and she imagined he'd just come from a break where he would have eaten an orange. Did he realize even the way his hands peeled the skin from an orange could turn a woman inside out?

Katie sucked in a slow breath, afraid to move. She worried he would kiss her as much as she worried that he wouldn't. She was in a mood tonight, and watching the play stations hadn't helped but instead stoked the flames inside her until, now pressed against one of the men of her nightly dreams, she wanted nothing more than to submit to his every whim. She ached with the desire to be touched, to be tied, and to be fucked by Quinn and Leo.

He edged a little closer, but instead of kissing her like she expected, he stroked her lips with his tongue. A gentle touch that was more like a taste than a kiss. He leaned into her until they were pressed together from hips to breast, and his erection was unmistakable pushed against her belly and pelvis. His hot tongue licked at the corner of her mouth and along the seam of her lips. She opened farther on a soft sigh but he only continued his exploration.

Her own arousal went off the charts as she rolled her hips against his. A low growl sounded in his throat and he pulled his head back from hers. "Careful, Katie. For a girl who professes to being happy alone, your body is quickly making a liar out of you."

She clamped her mouth shut and tried to pull back, but there was nowhere to go. He had her against the railing and his arms still held her in place. "I think we should stop this, people are starting to stare."

Quinn glanced to the side, looking at the crowd surrounding them. "Since when do crowds bother either of us? That's common around here and no one really cares what we do. In fact, they probably wish we would do more. I think inside everyone here lies the heart of a voyeur."

She couldn't argue with that. Even she got excited watching some of the activities going on in the private play area. Especially the flogging. It had been so long since a flogger kissed her skin she might not remember the sensation, but every time she came to the club and watched, she got turned on as hell seeing the red streaks on bare flesh after a session in a booth. She enjoyed every flinch and emotion that crossed the faces of the submissives.

She loved the crackling sound of leather slapping a bare back or bottom. Oh yeah, she had it bad tonight, and there was never a shortage of people willing to put on a show.

"I can admit I enjoy watching, but I'm not sure I want to be the one on display."

The corner of his mouth turned up in a wry smile at her words. "We'll see about that." He pushed away from her and grasped her hand. "Come with me."

She looked down at his hand covering hers. The heat and desire enveloped her further from the simple movement. His rope roughened hands scraped against her wrist, igniting a flame deep inside her belly, the kind of thing that she hadn't felt in a very long time.

"Where are we going?"

"I have to get back to work and I don't want you far. I wasn't kidding when I said it was time."

Not giving her a chance to answer, he turned and pulled her into the crowd. Warm and pulsing bodies rubbed against her as they made their way through the throng of people clustered around the play stations. When they passed by the last St. Andrew's cross, a glance to the left showed her a new girl getting flogged by Dan, a Dominant who more than knew what he was doing. She was bare from the waist up and there were a variety of red, criss-crossing welts on her naked back. Despite Quinn leading her, she slowed her pace enough to take a look at the girl's face. Her black hair partially covered her features, but Katie managed to catch a glimpse of cobalt blue eyes glittering with tears. Despite the tears, or because of them, the naked emotion glowed from her face.

Katie's breath hitched in her throat when their gazes locked, and she understood exactly the ecstasy the woman experienced. With the dazed look in her eyes and the relaxed state of her body as she hung cuffed to the cross, it became obvious she was far beyond the simple pleasure of the leather striking her skin. She'd made it to the happy place affectionately called sub space.

A surge of envy rushed through her as she tore her gaze from the girl and refocused on Quinn in front of her. His sandy brown hair just brushed his shoulders and curled at the ends, and she imagined it to have a silky texture that would glide through her fingers like water. The snug black t-shirt that he wore hugged his broad shoulders and back before tapering down to disappear into the dark jeans wrapped around a tight ass and legs. That picture alone was enough to make any girl drool. She'd had her eye on Quinn for a very long time.

As they approached the stairs that would take them down to Leo and the ropes, her belly fluttered with nerves and an obvious case of fear. She really wasn't sure if she could do this, especially here in front of so many people who knew her as a regular.

When she first came to the club, she had wanted to learn more about the lifestyle and even dared to hope that she would find someone who might want to teach her. And learned she had, by watching and even sometimes suffering through her own arousal to all the stimuli in the room. But other than the staff, who had been warm and friendly to her, not a single man had approached her.

Looking at many of the beautiful, rail thin women of the club, she'd been forced to admit that her plus-size figure might not measure up for most of the men here. But she had no intention of letting that deter her from enjoying the atmosphere of the club and spending a few hours a week with like-minded people who at least wouldn't consider her thoughts and desires perverse or disgusting like her ex did.

"Katie, are you okay?"

She jerked her head up, surprised to find herself standing next to Quinn and Leo's private table and Quinn's gaze boring into hers with concern.

"Yeah—uhm—I'm fine." She tamped down her nervousness as best she could and gave him a small smile.

"Good, then you can sit here and watch while you wait, if you would like."

She looked at the table of women all waiting for their turn at the ropes and her stomach fluttered all over again. She didn't want to be one of their groupies, she just wanted to watch. This up close and personal, she didn't think she could hide just how turned on she would get. Nor did she want to be compared to the bevy of women who hovered here, hoping they would get picked next.

"Quinn—I'm not so sure—"

He pressed his fingers to her lips to quiet her words. "I am sure and Leo is sure. You have to start trusting sometime, Katie." With that he turned and walked over to the platform to join Leo in tying up their latest volunteer for the swing. Leo glanced over to her and smiled at Quinn with the wickedest looking grin she had ever seen. The kind of *oh, shit* look that made her realize how serious they were about this.

****

Two hours later, Katie still waited at the

table but had begun fidgeting in the chair. Her fingers tapped out the rhythm of the song playing through the club against the edge of the table, and her gaze darted everywhere in an attempt to not look at the ropes. Quinn and Leo had tied girl after girl without another word to her and her patience had run out. She wanted to either scream in frustration about being left waiting so long or stomp from the club like a child. She'd told Quinn that she wasn't ready for this yet, but he and Leo had apparently been discussing her at length. She'd watched and waited for weeks and couldn't be more surprised that they'd done the same. But this waiting was killing her.

She wanted to let her guard down and give them a chance, but the longer she sat there thinking about it the more she wanted to bolt. Doubts continued to plague her as she watched each new girl approach them. Why would they want to be the ones to teach her? It had been far easier to stay on the sidelines at a good distance and just observe. She glanced down at her cell phone for the umpteenth time to check the clock. Things would be winding down before long, so maybe they wouldn't put her on display. She could hope.

Earlier in the evening when she walked through the VIP doors, the first person she'd noticed was Leo leaning against a barstool dressed in a navy blue tee and looking through the crowd with a watchful eye. She couldn't resist staring at him. She'd heard many women in the club say that his bald head and tribal tattoo around his neck made him look scary. She couldn't disagree more. The man was sexy as sin from top to bottom. Given half the chance, she'd rub all over him like a cat in heat.

When he caught her watching him she had immediately become self-conscious. Maybe wearing her new slim skirt and a simple black corset hadn't been such a great idea. She had decided to leave her hair down tonight, thinking the red of it against the pale color of her skin and the dark as night corset would look good. She brushed her hands down the fabric covering her torso—she loved the new corset she'd bought. It made her feel feminine, not to mention it took several inches off her waist. If she hadn't known better she could have sworn the look in Leo's eyes said she looked good enough to eat.

"You look really nervous sitting there. Have you never done this before?"

Katie looked at the woman sitting across the table. "No, this is my first time."

"You don't have anything to worry about. Quinn and Leo there know just how to handle a woman."

The way the words rolled from the woman's mouth sounded like experience, and sexy as hell. The dreamy look in her eyes as she watched the two men grated on Katie's nerves. She so didn't belong here.

She glanced again at the time, then at the tiny blonde woman with enormous silicone tits that were completely bare except for two X's of black tape covering her generous nipples. The club would be closing soon, making the blonde the last customer of the night.

So much for it being her time.

She shook her head and turned back to the woman at the table. "Yes, I just bet they do."

The woman must have caught the sarcasm in her response because she swung her head to look at Katie with a sharp, laughing look in her eyes.

"They have been eyeing you for a long time, sweetie, just waiting for you to be ready."

"Uh huh."

She flashed a quick smile. "You have no idea what you're in for, do you? Well, I guess it doesn't really matter. They'll be sure to let you know when they are good and ready. The question you have to ask yourself is, are you ready?" She stood and walked away from the table and up to Leo and Quinn. She kissed them both soundly on the mouth and told them good luck. She stopped again at the table on her way to the door. "Tonight you are the envy of every woman in the club."

She walked through the exit, leaving Katie in a state of shock.

Leo leaned over the girl attached to the rope swing between them and spoke to Quinn. Whatever he said made him look over at her, and she fought not to squirm under his gaze. Quinn laughed and left the platform and headed directly for her.

11

Uh oh.

He dismissed the other women at the table and seated himself next to Katie.

"Having fun?" He took a swig of water from the bottle he'd left on the table earlier.

"Not really. Your groupies are the most boring women I have ever met. Although just calling them women is a stretch."

He couldn't hold back a smile on that one. She'd hit the nail on the head and not even he could deny it. Not many women who came to Purgatory and lined up for the rope swing were really all that affected by the touch of the rope, at least not that she could see. Instead they were just looking for a cheap thrill.

"Leo and I have learned to tune them out. You do get used to it after a while." He leaned in closer, enough to whisper in her ear. "You're fidgeting, Katie. Why?"

"I thought you brought me down here to be tied into the swing."

"You thought we were going to do that here?" Leo's voice sounded from over Quinn's shoulder.

"Well—uhm—yeah, I guess so." Feeling embarrassed, she hoped her face wasn't as red as she thought.

"I might not have been completely clear as to when…"

"What do you mean?" She whispered the question, anger filling her as she spoke. She uncrossed her legs and moved to stand—it was time to go. She'd thought to offer them her submission, but for some reason they simply wanted to humiliate her.

Leo placed his hands on her shoulder and took the seat behind her. "Your first time shouldn't be in public, but it should be now and with us. Do you really want to deny it? You should probably think about that before answering me. I expect you to be honest with yourself as well as with us. Anything else will be met with punishment."

Katie's cheeks flushed hot at Leo's words as she stumbled with a response. "I—I—would never be dishonest."

"That's not what I meant and you know it, sweetheart. You have a good heart, but you hide behind your wall. You want to submit but you won't open yourself up to it." Leo's fingers tapped along her shoulders, rubbing the bare flesh. "But that's what we're here for. We are both going to ask a lot of you tonight, are you prepared for that? Do you want it?"

Her gaze lifted and met Quinn's directly as she struggled with the irritation and fear. His laughter had been replaced with an intensity that took her breath away and made it difficult to look at him.

Katie glanced again at Quinn but focused on Leo touching her. She'd waited so long to hear the words, she wasn't sure she could believe them. Yes, she wanted them, but would she ever be the same again afterwards?

Leo was right, though, her own issues prevented her from giving in and really she just needed to relax and live a little.

"I'm scared."

"If you weren't I don't think either of us would be talking to you. We both take your submission very seriously." Leo continued to massage and stroke her shoulders and she damn near melted into his skillful hands, it felt so good. They'd kept her on edge for hours and she'd soaked her panties in anticipation of their touch. Now here they were, and they were giving her one last chance to back out. She wasn't going to take it.

"I'm sure." Her quiet, simple statement brought out a wicked grin on Quinn's face, and Leo pressed his lips to the back of her neck while his hands continued to roam her arms and torso.

"I can't wait to get you out of this corset and tie you up for myself." Leo's words sent a quick pulse straight to her already tight nipples and renewed heat pooled between her thighs.

When Quinn leaned forward and placed his hands on her knees, she nearly shot out of the chair. His touch electrified her.

"Spread your legs for me, Katie," he demanded.

Surprised by the sudden changes of the two men, she hesitated before letting her legs fall slightly apart, giving Quinn the access he sought. Grateful she'd taken the time to pamper her body before she came to the club, she held her breath as his fingers slid up her thighs and underneath the hem of her skirt.

"Are you wet, sweetheart?" She shivered at the kiss of Leo's warm breath on her skin as he spoke to her again, trying to distract her from the fact that Quinn was scant inches away from her pussy.

"Yes." Her husky answer gave away just how aroused she was, but did little to relieve the tension building or the wanting for them to hurry up and get on with it. In fact, she was beginning to care less and less about being in public, which gave her a better understanding as to why so many submissives in the club went so far in their play with others watching. At some point during the play there comes a time, she knew, when you don't care about anything but feeling. Something that no amount of research or observation could make someone understand.

She closed her eyes and held her breath when Quinn grazed the soft fabric between her legs. She bucked her hips toward his hand and a small groan escaped her lips.

"Oh yeah, Leo, she's ready. So fucking wet and hot." His fingers pushed aside her panties and slid through her slick folds, glancing across her swollen clit. She whimpered in pleasure as Leo grabbed her chin and twisted her head to the side so he could capture her lips in a hungry and demanding kiss. Pleasure arrowed through her as one man teased her clit and the other kissed her senseless. Losing focus, her instincts took over and her body began to build toward an orgasm. When she didn't think she could hold it back, she tore her mouth from Leo and pleaded for more.

"No, baby, not yet." With that statement Quinn gave her clit a hard little pinch that took not only her breath but also quelled her impending orgasm. Moments later she panted for air and her eyes watered with threatening tears. "Just breathe, Katie, in through your nose and out of your mouth. Open your eyes and look at me."

She did open her eyes and looked around to see several people watching her display before settling her gaze on Quinn. Her body flushed hotly with embarrassment as he withdrew his hand and resettled her skirt back in place.

"I think we're done here and it's time to go home." For a minute she thought Leo meant they were done with her and wanted her to go on her way, but then he stood and grabbed her hand to pull her along with him. "Give your keys to Quinn so he can follow us with your car, you're going home with us."

She didn't argue, she couldn't. Her body raged with need and a desire for these two men like never before. She figured even one night of pleasure with the elusive men would last her a very long time, and she wasn't about to turn it down.

****

Surprised by how quickly they arrived at their place, she became fascinated with the one-room loft in the industrial area of downtown. The large space was essentially split in half with a small open-air kitchen and large living area filled with leather couches and chairs and enough electronics to make any Best Buy geek jealous. At each end of the room were large, king-sized beds covered with black suede comforters and a couple of chest of drawers. The walls were covered with framed black and white prints of women in various states of undress and tied in every possible position an imagination could think of.

But it was the idea that the two of them lived together with no privacy from the other that intrigued her the most. She'd often wondered if they were lovers as they seemed so in sync with each other, not to mention all the stories she'd heard about them sharing women when they played. Did they share each other when there weren't any women around? An image of their naked bodies writhing on one of those beds together flashed through her mind and she let out a low moan.

"Are you okay, Katie?"

She jerked her head to meet Quinn's gaze as her heart beat faster at being caught in a dark fantasy she wasn't about to share with anyone.

"Hmm. Wouldn't I like to know what you were just thinking of? "

"I'm—uhm—no." She pushed those crazy thoughts from her brain and concentrated on her surroundings once again. "Nice place you have here. Suits you both."

"Thanks, we like it." Quinn led her further into the loft, next to the seating area. Leo took a seat on one of the couches directly in front of her and Quinn walked around behind her, leaving her to face Leo with him at her back. His fingers went to the laces of her corset and slowly began to loosen them. Her body heaved a sigh of relief as she inhaled a deep, relaxing breath.

"That's it, Katie, relax and let Quinn work his magic."

She loved the rough, dark timbre of Leo's voice—its inherent power soothed her rough edges. She smiled and continued her deep breaths.

"Yes, Sir."

"Now that's more like it." His hands rubbed against his jeans-covered thighs slowly, up and down their length. Her gaze immediately went to the growing bulge in his lap, which she tried to avert her eyes away from but couldn't. Instead she thought only of kneeling there on the floor before him and freeing his erection so she could suck him. Her mouth watered with desire to know his taste. To feel his hand on her head as he fucked her mouth.

Oh, dear God, she was so horny.

"We know you've heard of safe, sane, and consensual. Do you have a safe word?"

She shook her head.

"Okay then for tonight you will use the word 'red.' If you use it, all play will stop. Understood?"

"Yes, Sir." Although stopping was the furthest thing from her mind.

Quinn drew out her laces one by one before he finally finished releasing her from the corset and whisked it off her body and tossed it into an empty chair. Cool air rushed across her skin and her nipples pebbled instantly. Strong, masculine fingers traced the indented curve of her waist before sliding up her rounded stomach to cup a plump breast in each hand. She sighed in pure ecstasy at his touch.

"Have you ever had your breasts bound?"

"No." Her answer came out barely a whisper. She found it hard to talk when she couldn't even think. Her body felt like it was on fire and her pussy creamed harder in response. The scent of her heat filled the air around them and she was certain they could both smell it.

"There are so many ways I can work the rope around you, it's hard to pick just one." Leo's fingers pulled and strummed her aching nipples as he spoke. A sigh escaped her lips as she arched into his hands, praying he wouldn't stop.

"Take off your skirt." With shaky fingers she fumbled with the button and the zipper before shimmying the skirt down her hips and thighs. Leo scooped her skirt from the floor and tossed it out of the way.

"Do you have a favorite design?" She suspected that some of the Shibari patterns would be, and she could imagine how sensual he would make her look and feel tied up in one.

His hands dropped to her side and he took a step away from her. She looked at Leo in alarm, who with a simple look reassured her everything was fine.

Quinn walked over to a tall cabinet in the corner and opened the front panel to reveal row after row of coiled rope in every color imaginable.

"This is our private rope collection, Katie. Each one has been hand colored with a specific person or design in mind. He reached in to the top shelf and removed an exquisite magenta colored strand and moved back toward her. "This is the one we designed specifically for you, babe. We've been saving it."

"You were that sure of me?" Quinn merely smiled. "You planned tonight?"

"We've been planning tonight for a long time, sweetheart. We just had to wait until we thought you were ready."

She shivered a little from the cold and from the confidence that these two men had in her. Could she possibly live up to it? "And you think I'm ready now?"

"Yes." They replied in unison.

Quinn unfurled the rope and draped it over her shoulders. The dark burgundy color against her fair skin stood out stark and beautiful. They were right about it being a good color for her.

Her favorite dress was in that exact shade. In fact, last month she'd worn that sexy outfit to the club and Leo had complimented her on it.

Leo stood from the couch and paced toward

her, stopping mere inches from her nude body. His fingers grabbed the edges of the rope and pulled her forward against him as he slanted his mouth across hers. His tongue plunged through her lips, taking her with an unexpected hunger. Her own body responded as she rubbed against him, spreading her legs just enough for the rough fabric of his pants to scrape against her clit. She moaned into his mouth as he pulled the rope tighter, forcing it to dig into the skin on the back of her neck.

Hands grasped at the globes of her ass, spreading them, and a finger ran along the crack. She'd never had two men touching her at the same time, and their attention was a heady sensation as they pinched, pulled, and prodded her sensitive spots. Every movement came with a spark of both pain and pleasure as they experimented with her body.

When Leo pulled from her lips she wanted to beg and plead for more, but she instinctively knew better. Two experienced Dominants working her body were only going to give her what they wanted and nothing more. She had to be patient. He tied a knot into the rope at her throat, which rested in the hollow like a necklace. Leo continued to make a series of knots at short intervals all the way to the apex between her thighs.

Quinn's hands moved across her back and under her arms to her front. When he wrapped a separate section of rope between the knots that Leo had tied and pulled them tight around her back, it created a diamond pattern on her chest. He tied off the rope and repeated the process with each new section until she had a series of diamonds trailing down her torso straight to her pussy. Occasionally the last knot rubbed against her clit, causing her to lose her breath and focus every damn time.

With a wicked smile Leo bent down to pull the rope between her legs. She'd seen this pattern before and she knew they would attach the rope work in the front to what Quinn had done in the back and, oh dear God, that rope would nestle between her folds and run up her ass to her back.

Already her body flamed hot. The scrapes and tugs of the ropes against her skin drove her mad, and she just knew that if that knot rubbed her just a little bit more she would explode.

On the verge of begging to come, Katie cried out when Leo buried his face between her legs. His tongue speared the slick, heated folds, licking at her juice but not touching her swollen clit. Instead he slid downward and plunged his tongue inside her as deep as he could get it. Her head lolled backwards against Quinn's chest as he braced her arms with his hands to keep her from falling.

"Whatever you do, Katie, don't come without permission."

Was he kidding? She wanted to scream in frustration as she tried to wriggle away from Leo's tempting tongue. Her attempts to stop him were futile. He simply grabbed her ass and held her tight against his face, while he continued to work her pussy with his hot tongue. She wanted to cry. Their demand for her to not come under these conditions was unreasonable. She wouldn't—couldn't hold back.

"I—I can't stop it. Please, please, it's..."

Her words died as Quinn pinched her nipples so hard it took her breath away. The demanding need to come died with the onset of such sharp, unexpected pain. Tears sprang to her eyes.

"Don't worry, babe, if you can't control it, I will." His firm words settled around her like a blanket. He and Leo had every intention of taking their pleasure as needed but, just as important, they would take care of her. In that moment they were everything to her and that warm feeling not only eased her pain but left her with the desire to please them like never before.

With a few last frenzied licks to her over sensitized tissues, Leo not only brought her right back to the brink of orgasm but he pulled away from her then, denying her a release.

Her gaze latched onto his at the sight of him licking his lips. "Such a good girl. Tastes good too," Leo spoke as he threaded the rope between her soaked flesh, turning it over to Quinn, who pulled it tight enough so that the texture of the rope touched every sensitive spot she could think of. Quinn settled the last knot snugly against her hard little clit.

If she moved even a tiny fraction, teasing

pleasure fractured through her, which was designed precisely to drive her crazy. When the rope was secure, Quinn delivered a sharp little blow to her ass. "Now the real fun can begin. But first, don't you want to see how gorgeous you look now? Tied just for us?"

"Yes." It was all she could manage. Even deep breathing moved the rope enough to excite her.

He grabbed her hand and pulled her behind him. A gasp of pleasure forced its way from her mouth with each step. The simple movement of one step in front of another moved the tight rope along her pussy and ass, a constant press and release of pure bliss that made it difficult to think.

"Feels so good, doesn't it?" She nodded. "You're not going to come until I tell you to, right?"

"Yes, Sir."

He stopped her in front of a full-length mirror that gave her a first glimpse of her rope-clad body. Normally a little self conscious about her nudity, what they'd done to her, the beautiful rope work, made her proud of the way she looked.

"Oh my God, it's stunning!" She tried to fight back the tears that welled in her eyes, but a few leaked out anyway. "You've made me so beautiful."

Both men stepped closer and embraced her between them.

"No, Katie, you were already beautiful

beyond measure, we just showed you how much."

"I don't know what to say," she whispered. "Thank you."

"Don't thank us yet, let's see how you feel when we are done playing with you."

A healthy dose of fear shot through her, but not enough to bring her back from the euphoria they had created. She felt so good right now, she almost didn't care what they did as long as she got to come soon.

"Do you still remember your safe word?" She nodded. "What is it? I need you to say it."

"Red."

"Okay then, go get up on that bench then and get down on all fours for us, baby."

She looked over to where Leo pointed and saw a black leather padded bench only a few feet away. She took a deep breath to steady herself because she knew even a few feet of movement could be enough to make her come, and she couldn't do that until they said.

She moaned with agonizing pleasure when she moved toward the bench, the continued rubbing against her sensitive flesh almost more than she could bear.

Her steps faltered. "Please."

"Almost, baby. Just do as you're told and we'll take care of you. Trust in that." She heard the rustling of clothes being removed behind her as she took the last few steps and got into position as requested. With her ample ass high in the air and nothing to cover herself, feelings of vulnerability mixed with pure decadence washed through her. She watched both men approach her, Leo carrying a crop and Quinn a wicked grin.

She stared at their erections in awe. More heat spiked through her as she waited for them to touch her. Two gorgeous but drastically different men. Together they both wanted her, and everything she had dreamt of was coming true.

Quinn stepped in front of her and laced his hands through her hair. "You really have been such a good girl and I think you deserve a reward. Open wide, baby." He placed the tip of his cock against her lips and she opened her mouth, more than eager to taste him. She stroked the head of him with a long, slow lick before swirling along the more sensitive underside. His masculine heat and taste exploded on her tongue as she delved farther along the shaft with her mouth, his thick length stretching her lips around him. A deep, sexy groan from Quinn filled the quiet space of their apartment.

More. She wanted more.

So distracted by the luxurious feel of Quinn's dick in her mouth, she'd forgotten for a moment about Leo behind her until she felt the touch of a small, cool strip of leather against one bare ass cheek. He caressed circles along her skin and took his time going back and forth from one globe to another. His hand grabbed the rope that ran along her ass and pussy and she nearly came with a jolt.

She needed to beg again, but it was impossible to talk with Quinn's cock stuffed in her mouth, and his hands in her hair holding him all the way to the back of her throat. Katie relaxed her throat and did her best attempt to swallow against his flesh.

"Fuck!" His hands tightened in her hair and the muscles in his body visibly tensed. "Our little girl and her dirty little mouth are going to make me come soon."

She reveled in the pride his words gave her until a sharp crack across her bottom shot an intense piercing pain throughout her backside and straight to her clit. It hurt—oh God, it hurt— but damn if she didn't want him to do it again.

A deeper burning built in her womb as her inner muscles jerked in response. Before she could consider how to control it, another blow from the crop landed on the opposite cheek. Her mouth tightened around Quinn on a low, deep wail. He was going to make her come and she wouldn't be able to stop it this time. Pleasure seared through her until she thought she was burning alive.

"Oh yes, Katie, suck my fucking cock."

Spurred on by his words, she worked him harder and faster. Leo's hands did something with the rope behind her as it fell away from her pussy. The release of the pressure against her clit and ass should have given her a measure of relief, or an ability to control the building orgasm, but it didn't. It was too late.

Quinn thrust in and out of her mouth in a rapid, frenzied pace. Pushing his dick a fraction deeper in her throat each time. Pleased with the wildness of his actions and desperate to taste him, to have all of him inside her, she tightened her mouth and stroked her tongue at the same pace he fucked her mouth.

"Fuck. Yes. Baby!" His words were short and clipped with agony until she felt a blast of hot semen cross her tongue. She didn't—couldn't—stop or slow as she continued to suck him as he filled her mouth with his release, eager for every drop.

"My turn."

With one long and deep thrust, Leo plunged his cock into her juice-soaked pussy. She cried out around Quinn as she was stretched and filled to capacity. He immediately withdrew to the tip and sank back into her body with just as much force.

"Give it to us, Katie, it's ours. Your come is ours now."

She couldn't quite comprehend Quinn's words. Not with Leo's cock pounding into her, building an intensity that was completely out of her control.

"Say it, Katie," Quinn demanded

"Please. Please. I can't—"

"Say it or he'll stop."

Her body bucked with every stroke, and she was lost in arousal. Fingers touched her breasts, her back...everywhere.

"Ours." Leo snarled the word.

"Yes!" she screamed out to them, so desperate now. "Both of yours." A finger pressed against her clit and her body exploded.

Fracturing her into tiny bits of light and pleasure as her body rocketed against them in spasms.

Her legs and arms weakened, unable to support her any longer. She reached out for something to hold onto and grabbed the railing in front of her.

She cried out over and over again as the strongest release of her life quaked over her. Her pulse beat with the ever increasing volume of the music until finally a bit of reality began to sink in again.

Wait a minute. What am I holding on to? She pried her eyes open to find herself standing at the railing in the club. She glanced around to the hundreds of people around her. Most of them didn't see her, but a few watched her with curiosity, some with blatant desire if she wasn't mistaken.

Oh. My. God. No!

Heat and humiliation coursed through her as she realized that she had just orgasmed right here in front of all these people while lost in a daydream about Leo and Quinn. She wanted to run and hide from the embarrassment. How could this happen to her, she hadn't even been drinking.

Leo and Quinn.

They were just below her. She'd been

29

watching Leo tie up another girl. She looked straight ahead at the stage, too afraid to look down. She had to get out of here. She would have to force herself to walk through the crowded club all the way to the exit and pray no one said a word to her. But first...she had to look down. Had to know if they'd noticed. Surely not. They were always so busy.

She took a deep calming breath and released on a nice slow exhale. She tilted her head down and looked. They both stood there, ropes in hand, staring up at her. Her gaze connected with Quinn and then with Leo. They both stared at her with such intensity and arousal that she thought the heat and embarrassment flushing her face would kill her.

Quinn was first to break into a smile. A grin so wide there was no mistaking just what they had witnessed.

Leo crooked his finger at her and motioned for her to come down. She wanted to duck and hide, but something deep within her wanted them more. She was a grown woman, and she could handle the fact that she had just had an orgasm in public. Hell, this was a fetish club, after all, and that kind of thing happened all the time here.

Just not to her.

She hesitated and Quinn's expression grew serious and mouthed one word to her. The one she'd waited for.

"Ours."

Displayed

Chapter One

"Em, are you really going to go through with this?" Katie yelled over the loud music pounding through the club.

"Of course I am. It's what I've been working up to for months now. Why would I back out now?"

"Oh, I don't know. Because maybe when you take off that mask and Rio gets one look at the real you, you'll be a dead woman."

Em looked at her friend's frightened expression, trying not to laugh. It had taken a long time getting to know the people here at Purgatory before she'd built up the nerve to tell anyone who she really was. Now she was tired of hiding, and ready to unveil her identity once and for all. She didn't want to think about the public humiliation Rio could put her through if he made a scene. She worried too much about him as it was.

"You know they don't allow masks at the private after-hours party. If I want to take the next step in my journey, and I do, then I have no choice but to reveal myself. Rio be damned." If the man wasn't already damned. She looked up at where he stood, watching one of the play stations. Master D's station, of course. She couldn't tell what he was doing tonight, but she knew it was one of the more hardcore stations they offered where they did things like violet wand or needle play.

From this vantage point, she stared at Rio's profile. Wavy dark hair, tanned skin from working outdoors with her brother, and all black leather—from the vest to the pants that hugged what she knew was the most perfect ass on the planet, to the black leather boots he wore on his feet.

Here in this environment, he made it impossible to read his body language. She found him guarded, more often than not with a stern expression. Some went so far as to refer to him as El Diablo, the devil himself.

"Em, last dance of the night and I have a slot center stage with no one to fill it. You want it?" Gabriel, the club manager, had sneaked up behind her while she ogled Rio for the umpteenth time that night. She tore her gaze away and turned to Gabe with a smile on her face.

"You want me?"

"Ahh, my dear, you have no idea. Everyone wants the elusive Em."

"I find that hard to believe."

"Why is that?"

She shrugged. She wouldn't get into her

insecurities with Gabe. Here in the club things were different for her. She wasn't the sweet little Emerson whom no one ever spoke to.

No, here she was bold and wanton, and reveled in the attention of the many patrons who liked to watch her. Even Rio. He'd been cool about it, of course, never showing too much interest, but there'd been a few times where she'd caught his gaze as he watched her play. She'd thought the heat in his eyes matched the arousal coursing through her body at his perusal, but so far he'd been aloof, never approaching her.

"So, darlin', do you want to take the chains?"

She'd been eyeing that platform for a long time, wondering what it would be like to get up there, helpless in front of everyone.

"Yes, actually I do." Already her body hummed with anticipation. What better way to kick off the rest of her night than by putting herself out there in a new way?

"Come with me then and I'll get you set up."

She followed Gabe through the crowd as they headed for the cage in the middle of the room. The energy of it all vibrated through her core, turning her on. She'd certainly come a long way from the first night she'd stepped into the club. Gabe held his hand up and she allowed him to lead her onto the small stage.

Her stomach tightened, partly from nerves, but mostly excitement. She looked down at her outfit, grateful that she'd chosen to go bold and daring tonight. The miniscule leather skirt didn't quite cover her ass, and the fishnet halter-top allowed a peek at her nipples that were currently straining against the fabric.

"Raise your arms for me, Em." She did as he asked and he placed the manacles around her wrists, fastening her arms to the chains hanging from the top corner of the cage. Emerson spread her legs and allowed him to fetter her ankles as well.

"You comfortable?"

She nodded.

Gabe stood back and appraised her appearance. "You picked the perfect outfit for tonight. If I didn't know better, I'd say you had something like this in mind to begin with." Heat flared in his eyes as he reached for the hem of her skirt. For a split second his fingers flirted with the crack of her ass before he rubbed his palms down the back of her thighs and up again, lifting her skirt to reveal her bare bottom and get the show started.

The crowd around her roared their approval as a shot of excitement rushed through her chest and straight to her clit. Large, strong hands massaged her ass as her body writhed in tempo with his movements. God, she loved this. Her head buzzed with the rhythm of the music and the heady sensations of Gabe stroking her ass while everyone watched and chanted for more.

When Gabe pulled his hand away she didn't expect the loud smack across her skin that came next. The stinging pain caught her breath until his hand returned and smoothed the pain away.

"I'll bet your pussy's soaked right about now."

"Maybe." Hell yeah, she'd felt a liquid rush from the moment she'd stepped up to the platform.

"Ahh, darlin', your teasing days are over now, aren't they? If you stay for the private session, one of these Doms here tonight is going to show us all just how tasty you are."

Emerson's muscles jolted deep inside her. Gabe had no idea how much she longed to take her education and experience to the next level. As much as she wanted Rio to be the one to do it, she wasn't waiting for him anymore. It was now or never.

Another resounding smack on her opposite cheek brought her focus back to the here and now, and the crowd cheering in front of her. Automatically her hands fought at the bindings around her wrists, her mind shrieking for her to touch herself.

"Everyone in the VIP area is watching you right now. Speculating...planning. But don't worry. Dan came up with the perfect idea for your introduction tonight. Something more civilized than just fighting over you." Gabe's breath tickled the back of her neck every time he spoke, only increasing the madness building inside her—and he knew it.

"Who is watching me?" She couldn't see the area behind her and she didn't have the guts to ask him if Rio watched.

"Everyone." With a final smack to her ass, Gabe strode from the platform, leaving her body on fire and pulsating with the music. Just the way the patrons liked it.

Emerson bucked and swayed her hips to the beat of the music as the image of Rio standing behind her, staring at her, burned into her brain. This wouldn't be the first time he'd seen her naked butt in the club, but it was the first time she'd gone to the cage to be chained. From everything she'd heard, that's how he liked his submissives. Chained and helpless...

* * * *

Rio watched the mysterious Em's slender body sway with the music, her pale skin glowing in the ultraviolet lighting. His pulse pounded through his veins to the same tempo, and his dick pressed against his zipper so tight he thought he'd probably end up with a permanent imprint.

His fingers itched to trace the curved lines of her back, feel her sleek skin against his own. There were so many things he could do to her in that position, all designed to maximize her pleasure and feed on the energy of the crowd. If she were his, he would keep her like that as often as possible—on edge, ready.

For weeks he'd watched her grow downright daring, noting the clothes she wore to the play stations she visited, and how she finally allowed herself to be restrained in performance. Several times she'd caught him, and he could have sworn desire and something more had flared in her gaze—the same arousal he experienced every time he caught sight of her.

It was a shame he couldn't see her luminous eyes right now, although his imagination could envision them quite well. Slightly parted lips and flushed skin topped off with a look of longing not even he could deny. With each slow roll of her hips and tug on the cuffs at her wrists, his mouth watered and more blood rushed to his groin. She looked hot on display— every man in the place watched her with obvious lust in their eyes and thoughts in their heads of what they'd like to do to her.

Mine.

She threw her head back, arching her neck, and thrust her breasts toward the crowd. Fuck, the woman would have him crazed with longing before this little show was over. In that moment, he longed to stand behind her, feel between her legs, and see for himself just how wet she'd become. To whisper in her ear how he ached to fuck her. But he wouldn't do it, not before she begged.

What about her drew him so much? He'd heard through talk about her age, which made him uncomfortable and had been one of the main reasons he'd avoided talking to her. His needs ran dark, and from his past actions he'd learned the inexperienced weren't likely to fulfill them. Now, watching her stand there bound and open, he wondered if he'd been too hasty in his assessment.

From this view he could no longer see her hiding behind her mask. He ached to see more of her like this, free and naked, waiting for him.

Yeah, he had it bad when it came to Em, the secretive little minx who riled everyone up without even realizing it. Something tugged at the edge of his conscious as he surveyed the scene. Gabe stood not far from the stage, keeping vigil over her, probably dying to get a piece of her for himself.

So with all the interested players and her willingness to put herself out there, why the mask? What could she possibly be hiding that couldn't be revealed here? Purgatory was all about being yourself, free to be who you needed to be. Not to mention taking the opportunity to indulge in some fantasies, no matter how forbidden.

Time was ticking and his patience would only hold out so long. Soon he would have to find out.

Chapter Two

Twenty minutes later, Gabe returned and helped her down from the stage. Her legs and arms shook, and her pussy and nipples ached for attention. The fantasies she'd indulged in with the crowd watching left her ready to beg if she had to.

They crossed straight to the bar where Katie sat at one of the cocktail tables, waiting with a bottle of water.

"I've got her, Gabe, thanks."

"You sure? She's shaking pretty bad. She needs—"

"I've got her. Besides, you've got a club to close." Katie helped her to the chair and handed her the water. "Drink."

Em took the offered bottle and placed it to her lips, focusing on the cool water sliding down her throat and not the throbbing between her legs.

"You really get into that being on display thing, don't you?" Katie asked.

Emerson felt the heat creeping up her neck

and onto her cheeks, but she wasn't really embarrassed. How could she be when her blood flamed with arousal and her head spun from the attention?

"Yeah, I guess so." She panted. "I didn't know—didn't know it would be that intense."

"You've had Rio on the brain all night and that little trip pushed you over the edge."

Katie kept talking, but Emerson zoned her out, only thinking about hot hands on her ass, which she could swear she still felt. The music had stopped for a few minutes while the announcement of the club closing was made, but now it had returned and while the volume was lower it still held a driving, rhythmic beat that pulsed to her clit.

What would Rio say if she bent over this table and begged him to fuck her right here, right now?

"Are you even listening to me, Em?" Katie's voice pierced her wildly running thoughts with her stern tone.

"I can't stop...the music...the atmosphere."

"It's called subspace, Em, and you've lost your own ability to control the moment."

"I need to—God, I don't know what the hell I need."

"Yes, you do. You need to fuck, to get off, and right now you don't even care with whom."

"Rio."

"Isn't here right now, and I'm not going to let you face him or the coming party like this."

Emerson laid her forehead down on the table

and gulped for breath. The room needed to quit spinning.

"Em, do you trust me?"

"Of course I trust you."

"Enough to let me help you so you can recover?"

"Anything, please..." Soft fingers caressed her neck and massaged her shoulders. Katie was such a nice girl. Leo and Quinn better appreciate her.

She whimpered when Katie moved from behind her and took the seat next to her at the table.

"I'm going to touch you, Em, stay as calm as you can. Quiet, too, unless you want us both in trouble for sexual contact in a public area."

Em nodded. She'd do anything Katie wanted her to. Cool hands touched her inner thigh and the fingers traced a circle there, teasing her into relaxation.

"That feels good."

"I know it does, sweetie. Just trust me that I can help you and we'll have you back out there in time for the private festivities to begin."

Katie leaned into her until their bodies touched and Emerson relaxed into her soft, femininity. The scent of ripened raspberries hit her nose at the same time Katie's hand moved a few more inches up her thigh.

Awareness dawned and Emerson realized what would happen if she allowed Katie to keep going. Allowed, hell. Her body screamed to be touched, to find release any way it could get.

She raised her head to look at her friend and recognized arousal in her gaze as well as flushed cheeks and soft panting.

"Shhh. You don't have to say a word. In fact, I think the less that is said, the better."

Emerson nodded. She did trust Katie. She'd been kind and friendly to her since the first night, gently coaxing her to open up and relax. Showing her that at Purgatory all kinds were welcomed and accepted, no matter what.

She'd been envious of her at first, watching the way her two men doted on her even when they demanded her submission at times. The obvious love between them inspired her.

She wanted only one man, and no matter how she tried to purge him from her system, she couldn't. Tonight she would have him or not.

Emerson sucked in a deep breath when slender fingers grazed across her wet and swollen flesh, driving her closer to madness with each slow inch. Where she craved to be taken hot and hard, Katie moved at her own pace and took her time, drawing her into the action.

"Please Katie, more." Emerson buried her face into her friend's neck and inhaled deeply, loving the woman's clean and fruity scent.

"Don't worry, little one, we'll get there." Her voice took on a husky tone, giving away her own arousal. A fact she liked very much. She'd occasionally given thought to being with a woman, but had never been brave enough to explore it. Until now.

Emerson tilted her hips slightly, giving Katie better access to her sex, anxious for her soft touch to reach her clit.

"You are very impatient. I suspect that's going to get you into a little bit of trouble tonight. Patience is the toughest lesson to learn and always one of the first a Dom expects you to master."

She wanted to agree with Katie, but she really couldn't concentrate on the conversation with fingers moving between her pussy lips, increasing the tension already coiled tight within her.

Her breasts ached as well, and even the little strips of fishnet covering them was too much. She longed to be naked and splayed out, an offering to Katie's desires. What would Rio think if he saw her then? Would watching a woman get her off turn him on, or would he even notice?

God, she needed to get him out of her head. Why should everything she did be a reflection of Rio when he'd barely said two words to her here at the club, and little more than tease her when he saw her at home?

"Oh, hell." She moaned when Katie slipped her first finger inside her, pushing against the sensitive skin and nerve endings already hyper aware.

"Shhh, it won't do either of us any good to get kicked out of here tonight."

Emerson clamped her lips shut and gritted

her teeth against the need to scream when Katie added a second finger and increased the tempo of her movements. When she curled them inside her and rubbed against her G-spot, she practically jumped from the chair.

Her body shook with the new onslaught of sensations, and her head spun further as a rush of pleasure pulsed through her.

"Em, I'm going to touch your clit and I want you to come for me without screaming or making a sound. Do you understand?" The whispered command alone nearly threw her over the edge as she shook her head furiously.

Katie's fingers rubbed across her sensitive spot three more times and Emerson's muscles clamped around them, holding off her release until Katie touched her clit.

Two fingers latched onto one of her tight nipples and pinched and tugged at the same time her thumb pressed against her pulsing clit, sending an overload of fierce sensations racking through her body. Her lips pressed tightly together, she buried her face tight against Katie's skin as the mind numbing orgasm ripped through her body.

Emerson rode the fingers fucking in and out of her as the pain at her breast expanded her pleasure. When the waves engulfing her finally subsided, the tension in her body slowly released and she melted against her friend.

The pain at her nipple disappeared and Katie's hand eased from her body. "You are a beautiful and responsive woman, Em, and if Rio doesn't recognize that tonight, I might have to kick his ass."

Em glanced across the club at Leo and Quinn packing their gear. "What about them?"

Katie laughed. "I'm sure they know exactly what I'm up to and if they don't then I shall have to tell them."

Just then Leo glanced up, his gaze settling on Katie. Em swore the heat between them could set the place on fire. "I think Leo knows."

"Yep, and I foresee a devil of a punishment later."

"Oh no. I didn't mean to get you intro trouble. Maybe if I talk to him."

Katie covered her hand. "Don't even go there. You're my friend and I'd do anything to help a friend. Even take a delicious, drawn out flogging followed by a hard fuck."

Emerson laughed and turned her head. "Thank you, Katie."

"It was my pleasure, sweetheart, but if you're feeling able we should probably go and get cleaned up before the auction begins."

Nerves jolted anew in her stomach. In a moment of desperation she'd agreed to a big unveiling and auction as her introduction to the private group. It sounded like such a good idea, but what if Rio didn't want to buy her for the night? Emerson shook the negative thoughts from her head. If Rio truly didn't want her even now, then tonight she would move on.

Chapter Three

Rio walked into the third floor ballroom to a flurry of action at the stage in the middle of the room. "What's going on here?"

Ben, his friend and know it all Dom, turned and smiled. "You haven't heard?"

"Obviously not."

"We're inducting a new submissive into the group tonight and she has agreed to be auctioned for public play."

"Who is it, and why am I hearing about this now?"

"Apparently it was decided at the last minute.

"And?" He wanted to know who.

"It's that hot little thing who always wears a mask. I think they said her name is Em."

His stomach tightened. "We don't allow masks on this floor."

"That's the beauty of the whole thing. She'll wear her mask for the auction and then the winner will reveal her identity."

Rio's cock perked up instantly at the

remembered image of the masked Em in the cage tonight. Even in the smoky and darkened club he could make out her reddened cheeks from where Gabe had given her several good smacks on the ass as he'd worked her up for the crowd.

It wasn't the first time he noticed her, but her open and sensual response to the crowd tonight had really grabbed his attention. So far, she hadn't spent much time with any particular Doms at the club, but she had become braver each week with her clothing choices, and tonight she'd really opened up.

"What time is the auction?"

"Whenever the little honey gets that cute ass of hers up here." Ben moved in closer and lowered his voice. "I heard that her performance downstairs really got her off and she needed some help coming down."

"Some help?" He didn't like the sound of that.

"Yeah, Gabe offered his assistance but Katie pushed him away and took control of Em in the corner by the bar. I don't know what happened there, but boy, would I have enjoyed being a fly on the wall."

Rio nailed Ben with a hard glare. "You are such an ass sometimes."

"Yeah, and that's what the subbies love so much about me." He flashed a toothy grin. "Are you going to tell me that you aren't curious about what Katie did to bring Ms. Masked Hottie down from subspace?"

He was, but he wasn't about to share that with Ben or anyone else. When he didn't rise to the bait, Ben wandered closer to the auction floor as the crowd grew ever larger with anticipation. This was going to get interesting.

Gabe stepped up to the microphone and the noise in the room quieted down. "I know y'all have heard about the plan by now, so why don't we get our newest submissive in here and we can get this show on the road?"

Rio glanced at the door in the far corner and saw a small figure staring through a slight crack in the door. He'd bet the infamous woman of the hour was the one peeking in. He could imagine her standing there, biting her lip and tugging at the edges of her straight brown hair.

"The rules are pretty simple. We're doing this impromptu auction for the club's favorite charity and the beautiful Em has agreed to a public play scene within her club documented limits, of course."

A round of boos erupted from the crowd, followed by raucous laughter. Rio figured this little lady would fetch a pretty high price for the night.

"Oh, and don't forget at the close of the auction, the winning Dom will remove her mask right here on stage before any play begins in accordance with our club's policy."

Applause erupted, as did a few calls to get on with the show, and even Rio vibrated with an urgency he couldn't quite contain. He wanted to see who was behind that mask.

Eliza Gayle

"You going to bid tonight, Rio?" Ben couldn't seem to let this situation go.

"Don't know yet. I think I'll wait and see what the rest of you pervs do."

"Takes one to know one, I reckon."

"I guess so." He liked that even though Ben came across goofy at times, he didn't get all puffed up and put out at the slightest perceived insult. He couldn't tolerate that kind of crap.

Gabe leaned into the microphone and turned his head to the door. "Katie, hon, go ahead and bring her in."

More applause sounded when the door swung open and Katie stepped through, leading Em by the elbow. Now those riggers were some damn lucky men when they'd latched onto Katie. She was the epitome of a Dom's wet dream with her tight corset that cinched her waist and lifted her ample breasts to almost spilling over the top. Even now with her flushed face and bright smile, she would be breaking hearts all over again.

But it was Em who continued to draw his eye, and had for sometime. He guessed she only stood five-two, which was a far cry from his six feet. Her slender body fit her height, but the first time she'd pulled her skirt up in the club for a flogging, she'd revealed a perfectly round ass that pinkened to a glowing red against her pale skin when spanked.

He'd yet to get close enough to see the color of her eyes, but the ruby red tint of her full lips mesmerized him, making him wonder what she tasted like.

Katie released her arm as Em took to the steps and made her way across the platform to stand next to Gabe.

"Hey, sweetheart, how are you doing?"

"Fine." She spoke quietly but the powerful microphone picked up her voice. Hesitant. Sweet. Familiar. A memory tugged at him that he couldn't quite reach. Where could he know this delicate morsel from, and how could he possible have forgotten her?

"All right, men, Em here is ready. So let's start the bidding at fifty dollars."

Right away a man up front raised his hand and the bidding rocketed from fifty to five hundred in under a minute. Apparently Em was a popular girl here at the club.

"Did you gentleman see our darling here in the cage tonight?" Gabe bent and trailed his fingers from her knee to the edge of her skimpy skirt and they all watched a shudder rack through her. "It's been a long time since I've seen such a natural in public. Someone here is going to be one lucky man tonight. In fact, I think I might be jealous."

Catcalls and lewd suggestions flew through the crowd as Gabe worked them up for more bidding. His gaze traveled back to Em and he found her staring at him, not moving or looking around. Rio's cock thickened at the intensity and the determination he saw there, a trait that called out to him in challenge. Her body language spoke of pride in who she was, and the slightly parted lips and tight nipples reminded him how much she liked the attention of a public setting.

"All right, settle down, or I'm just going to keep her for myself."

A slight smile formed at the edge of her lips but her gaze never wavered. Whatever happened from here on out, for whatever reason, she had set her sights on him. As the bidding raced toward one thousand dollars his dick continued to grow under her perusal and she didn't flinch or blink for a second from his.

"How about we sweeten the pot, fellas?" Gabe leaned into her and whispered something in her ear and she nodded, giving her consent to whatever it was he wanted to do.

He spun her around, forcing her to look away, and ordered her to bend over. Not only did that move reveal the globes of her ass, it also exposed a bare pussy when he nudged her legs farther apart. Someone in the crowd handed him a flogger, which he trailed lightly across each of her cheeks.

"For each bid you place, she will receive one stroke against her bare bottom." Quickly several men threw out bid numbers and she received several strikes one right after the other.

At fifteen hundred the bids once again slowed and Gabe stopped long enough for everyone to see the red streaks already forming and the moisture collecting along the swollen lips of her cunt.

Rio couldn't take it anymore. Everything in

him wanted to be the one stroking the tender spots to soothe away her pain, to run his thick fingers through her slick folds until she begged him to end her torment.

"Two thousand dollars." His voice sounded broken but loud. Every head in the crowd turned to look at him. A few whispers broke out and Gabe stepped in front of the microphone asking for any more bids. Many of the men looked at each other and him, debating whether to bid against him. When no one stepped forward or spoke up, he declared Rio the winner of the night.

"Come and get your prize and let us all see what you have won."

Rio moved effortlessly through the parted crowd and hopped up onto the stage, moving to stand behind Em. As much as he couldn't wait to see her secret identity, he thought he'd play it up for the crowd. His fingers tugged at the secure tie holding her mask in place until it loosened. Her body stiffened and she held her breath.

"Don't worry, Em, this is what everyone has been waiting for." He pulled the mask away, letting it drop to the floor, and everyone in the room cheered.

"All right, everyone, the special auction is officially over. Let's play." Gabe strode from the stage and left him and Em standing together, waiting. Why all of a sudden had she frozen up, her back as stiff as a steel rod? She'd been playing to him as often as she could and tonight he'd finally bitten.

"Why are you so nervous?"

"I've been waiting for this for a very long time."

"The private party?"

"No." she hesitated and he waited. "You."

The newly formed pit in his stomach set off his instincts as alarms went off in his head. He was definitely missing something here. He jerked her shoulder and whipped her around, catching his first glimpse of her full face.

His heart stopped in his chest and blood pounded in his cock. His personal and very forbidden wet dream stood in front of him.

Emerson. Fuck.

Chapter Four

Emerson watched the rage build in Rio's eyes at her identity. She'd known this would not be easy but he looked like he might throttle her any second.

"What the fuck do you think you are doing, Emerson? Are you out of your mind?" he roughly whispered. Without giving her a chance to answer he grabbed her arm, his fingers digging into the flesh, and led her off the stage and into a small room off to the side.

She tried to jerk her arm out of his grasp, but he didn't let go. "What the hell does it look like I'm doing?"

"Playing games."

That stunned her. She hadn't thought he would be mean when he found out. Upset yes, mean no.

"I'm not playing any games, Rio. I'm an adult woman exploring her fantasies." She glared at him. "All of them."

His grip on her arm loosened and his thumb rubbed where he squeezed. The move seemed so automatic she wondered if he even realized he was doing it.

"You don't belong in a place like this."

"Why not? You're here."

"I'm not young and. naïve, either." Oh, he went too far on that one. He needed to stop treating her like a kid.

"I may be younger than you, but I sure as hell am not naïve. Or innocent or pure or any other ridiculous label you want to put on me."

"Your brother will kill us both if he finds out we're here together. I can't do this." He pushed his hands roughly through his hair, frustration lines forming around his mouth.

"Give me a break. I'm not twelve years old anymore, so you can't just pat me on the head and send me away again. If you don't want to be my Dom tonight, if I repel you that much, I will find someone else."

In a flash his hands circled her waist and hauled her against him. Every last hard inch of his chest, torso, and pelvis pressed against her, including the hard cock in his pants. Her pussy creamed again, betraying her anger.

"You will not find someone else," he whispered darkly. His lips hovered near her mouth as she struggled for breath. He had the ability to twist her up and turn her around so that she couldn't remember who she was, let alone what she wanted to say.

"I'm not leaving." He'd better not force her hand on this, his influence in the club could very well get her expelled. He continued to glare at her as the warmth of his arousal spread across her bare stomach. She'd often wondered what it would be like to wrap her hands around his thickness, maybe even slide it into her mouth. He couldn't just walk away now, could he?

Suddenly his mouth covered hers, rough and demanding. His tongue pushed between her lips and swept through her mouth, throwing her further off balance.

The deeper they went, the more she felt every inch of his thick shaft pressing against her. Any more and she would melt into a puddle on the floor.

He tore his mouth from hers. "There is no one else here for you. I shouldn't even be touching you. But God help me I can't stop now."

She wet her lips, stroking the swollen flesh of her mouth. "Why do you have to stop?"

His tongue licked at her bottom lip and she opened on a sigh, drawing him into her mouth and sucking on his tongue lightly. Her arms lifted and wrapped around his neck, more of his heat searing into her skin. She had waited so long for this moment, and had been willing to do anything to be naked and underneath him.

"You're just a kid, Emmy." She cringed at the name he used for her when she was little. He was never going to get past the fact that he was older than her and best friends with her brother. It was a barrier he wouldn't cross no matter whether he wanted to or not. She fought against tears that burned behind her lids. She couldn't cry...wouldn't.

She curled her fingers around his shoulders and shoved him away. "If you don't want me then stop torturing me."

Heat flared in his eyes, shifting his demeanor a moment before he moved. "You think this is torture? You haven't seen anything yet, babe." He grabbed her hand and pulled her from the room right into the crowd of partygoers. They were met with cheers and comments that sent heat rushing to her cheeks. They were still looking to watch her play.

Fat chance of that at this point. She'd be lucky if he didn't grab her by the hair and throw her out of the club. Probably would call her brother, too.

"You're sure this is what you really want, Emerson?" He spoke close to her, his warm breath caressing the skin and tickling her ear. Her heart raced and her nipples poked at the abrasive fishnet fabric encasing them.

"I'm sure," she whispered. What did he have in mind, was he going to fuck her in front of everyone? Her stomach clenched. There was no one anywhere she trusted more than Rio, even if he hovered on the edge of a foul mood. He would never physically hurt her, although the odds of a broken heart on her part were pretty high.

He led her over to an open room in the corner, mumbling something about consequences she chose to ignore. There was a door that could be closed for privacy, but he left it open. The wall facing out to the ballroom would have been almost entirely a window had there been a window in it. Instead it was a big square hole where the crowd could gather and watch.

Inside, the room was painted midnight blue with soft lighting that gave visitors and players plenty of light to see without being harsh. Extraordinary black and white erotic photos hung strategically around the room and black cabinets sat in each corner, filled with any toy or implement one could think of.

In the center of the room stood a custom made, leather covered horse. A real showpiece bench made for many wicked delights, she imagined. Not to mention the pain that could be implemented if that was her desire. They headed in that direction and she pictured herself tied down on top of it with her naked ass facing the window.

Rio pulled her past it, though, and instead led her to the cross nailed to the wall that had a low bench in a wide V shape. "Are you familiar with one of these?" he asked her.

She shook her head as the picture formed. There were hooks at the ends of the cross and on the bottom of the ends of the narrow seat.

"It's called a St. George's chair, perfect for a wanton girl like yourself. Remove your clothing and have a seat."

She hesitated.

He leveled a serious look at her. "Emerson,

are you going to be able to obey?"

She swallowed past the lump in her throat and settled her hands across her stomach to settle her nerves. "Yes, Sir." She untied her halter at her neck and back and let it fall to the ground at her feet. She then shimmied from her skirt and kicked it off her legs. Standing naked in front of him for the first time was both a thrill and nerve wracking. He paused a moment to look her up and down from head to toe, then headed over to the cabinet for supplies.

"Go ahead and sit."

Feeling slightly self-conscious, she did as told and turned and sat on the small seat with her back against the padded cross on the wall. When she looked up, she faced the open window and the huge crowd that had formed to watch. She'd heard their hushed whispers behind her back, but seeing them in front of her, not knowing how far Rio wanted to go, left her with a familiar nervousness tinged with excitement coursing through her veins.

He returned with several packages, which he placed on the table next to her. "Let me have your wrist." She held out her hand and watched him wrap her wrist with a black leather cuff lined with pink fur. He repeated binding her on the other side. Each cuff had a D-ring that attached to the fasteners at the far end of each side of the cross, so that her arms were straight out and basically attached to the wall.

"Ankles, now." He stood in front of her, temporarily shielding her from the crowd. His big hands caressed her knees while his mouth took her in a slow, drugging kiss. Em opened to him, hungry for what he gave. What surprised her was the obvious show of need from him with each thrust of his tongue. His passion took her breath away. She could get lost in attention like this. With her focus solely on his possession of her mouth, she barely noticed that his hands slid between her thighs and pushed her legs open until the cool air rushed across her now exposed labia. She moaned into his mouth, and he swallowed the needy sound.

He broke the kiss and went to work attaching her legs to the bottom of the chair. When he finished, he stood and walked to the table at her side. She now sat fastened down with her arms and legs spread open, her pussy on complete display to all who watched. There were many smiles and appreciative gestures in her direction and, despite her love for attention, her body heated.

"Emerson, look at me." She turned and met his gaze. "Are you frightened?"

Was she? She was certainly nervous but no, not scared.

"No."

Rio smiled that wicked grin, the one that said, I am going to devour you. "How did I know you were going to enjoy this?" He picked up a black cloth from the table and draped it across his hands. "You've been hiding from all of us for months, I think it's only fair that we hide from you this time." He wrapped the blindfold around her eyes, tying it in the back. Her hands strained against her restraints in automatic response to wanting to remove the blindfold.

"Are you sure you trust me, sweetheart?" The deep cadence of his voice relaxed her struggling. Of course she trusted him. She'd known him since she was a pre-teen with a silly crush.

"Yes, of course."

"You are a very brave girl." Without seeing his face she couldn't tell whether he was being sarcastic or not. She suspected he was.

With her vision removed, her other senses began to take up the slack. The voices at the window seemed to grow louder and she even heard Rio's deep but quickened breathing. She'd bet he was as excited by this event as she was. She longed to see his reactions, to touch his body, to know what he was thinking.

"Loss of control is hard for a first timer in a situation like this, so my job is to break through the barriers you are building and give you what you need. Like these breasts...so petite and succulent...and in great need of attention."

His hands massaged and stroked her small globes. When his fingers grazed her nipples she arched her back into his hands with a hiss of pleasure. With forefinger and thumb he pinched her tips until she sucked in a hard breath. Pain built alongside the pleasure.

"Try to be still for me, Emerson. This is all about control for both of us. You still have a lot to learn."

How could she be still when every touch and taste was designed to drive her crazy? She whimpered when his hands left her body and he moved away. The whispers of the crowd returned without him there to distract her. She made out the words tits and cunt several times. Liquid heat rushed to the folds of her pussy. God, even if she wanted to deny how much this turned her on, the evidence gave her away.

A new sound came from the direction of the little table and she realized that Rio had moved the stool she'd seen along the wall. Was he sitting on it? Would he be touching her again?

"Everyone loves your body, sweetheart. They want more...they want to see you come." Her head jerked at the close contact of his voice in her ear. She hadn't even heard him approach. "Do you want more? Or should I stop now and let you go?"

"No, don't stop." Her voice came out hoarse and louder than she'd expected, and a murmured appreciation came from the end of the room. A light stroke of her flat belly sent new shivers racing to her core.

"Relax, Emerson. You're supposed to enjoy yourself." She loved the dark timbre of his voice, it soothed her and allowed her to slowly release the tension in her shoulders and torso. When his fingers trailed through the wet slit of her sex, she tried to tilt her hips to encourage him and received a sharp slap to her inner thigh.

"You're not being still like I asked. Patience is what you need."

"Can't help it, need so much." She breathed heavily.

"I know, and you need to trust me that I understand these things. Trust me, Emerson. In fact, I am revoking your permission to speak. You will also have to remain quiet. Do you understand?"

She nodded. "Good girl. Now let me give everyone a good view of this pretty pink pussy of yours."

His fingers moved quickly, spreading her lips wide open. Besides the few whispers she heard, she also caught a few moans, both feminine and masculine.

"It's very lickable, wouldn't you say?" Her muscles clenched tight and her juices flowed at his words. She had longed to know what it would feel like to have Rio's mouth there, teasing her clit...tasting her.

The stool moved rapidly like it had been kicked out of the way, but she had no idea what he was doing. Footsteps...she heard several. Only Rio's, or were there others as well? His hands dropped away and she heard a package being opened on the table. Every muscle in her body had gone taut, unable to relax as she tried to anticipate his next move and the next touch to her body.

"I think this toy will be a good way to really get this part started." A buzzing noise started up and she knew he held a vibrator of some sort.

"Hold this for me, will you? And feel free to

give it a little test run on her if you like while I get the next implement ready."

Who the hell was he talking to? He wanted someone else to play with her as well? She didn't get much chance to think about it when the cool, vibrating toy was pushed against her nipple. The low buzz sparked a reaction deep in her body and the whimpers she'd managed to hold back came tumbling out.

"Very nice. I think she likes that." Another package opened as the vibrations went from one nipple to the other until the peaks tightened almost painfully. She heard a vague squirting noise in the distance and then a finger was touching her ass, poking at the small hole. She hadn't even realized the chair had left that part of her anatomy accessible.

"I'll bet you've never been taken there, have you?" Oh, God—the slick finger breached her hole and pushed against untouched nerve endings. "That's okay. I have just the thing to help that virgin ass." His finger pushed in a little farther and then withdrew. A gasp tore from her mouth at the change in sensation. Holy hell.

"Now, do your best to relax and push against the plug if you can. It will make getting it in all the easier." A cool, rigid shape pushed against the puckered hole Rio had lubricated in preparation. She sucked in a breath and relaxed on the exhale. She could do this.

Suddenly the vibrator was removed from her breasts and placed lightly across her clit, sending shards of pleasure streaking through her body as the plug slid into place in her ass, stretching and filling her.

"Oh, such a good girl you are. I think you deserve a reward." He snapped his finger and moments later a mouth latched onto each one of her breasts. She was quickly losing count as to how many people touched her. Now, teeth bit at her nipples just enough to give her that edge of pain that heightened the feel of the vibrator at her clit and the plug seated in her ass.

"You've become quite the star tonight, Emerson." She couldn't focus on his words. Sensations and pressure built inside her to the point she couldn't stop it. Her legs and arms shook with the need to come. Knowing that everyone in the room and at the window would watch only heightened her pleasure. With anyone else she might have backed out, but Rio would take care of her, she knew.

"Make me come, Rio. Please, I need you, please." She pleaded with him, wanting him to be the one to tip her over the edge. Her heart raced in the silence of the room as she struggled to wait for him. "Please," she whimpered.

When she'd about given up the fight, fingers plunged into her slick vagina. She thought she'd heard Rio swear but she couldn't be sure as the shocking arousal ratcheted higher than anything she'd ever experienced. In and out those fingers moved, spearing her, rubbing tissues already aroused until the combination of it all exploded in her body.

Muscles spasmed uncontrollably as her body jerked in response. Screams ripped from her throat and bounced around the room as the darkness enveloped her, leaving her shocked and shaken at the force of her release.

Cheers and applause erupted around her and Rio hastily removed her blindfold.

"Are you okay, Em?"

She blinked against the lights and focused in on his face in front of her. Unable to speak, she only nodded. Her head slumped forward and Rio caught her with his hands.

"It's okay, sweetheart, I've got you." Fingers pawed at the cuffs of her wrists and ankles and she opened her eyes again to see Gabe and Katie setting her free. When her body was loose, Rio scooped her into his arms and held her tight against his chest. His lips pressed against her forehead in a gentle caress.

"Show's over, folks. We need our privacy." With that he carried her through the archway that led to a private bedroom with no windows and closed the door behind him.

Her mind reeled from the emotions coursing through her as Rio laid her out on the bed. She'd been surprised to see Gabe and Katie sharing the scene with her, but grateful for it. Much better than with strangers.

He rubbed at all the sore spots from their session. First, his thumbs caressed the skin around her wrists in a light circular motion while the smooth slide of his tongue tormented the soft skin of a breast. Through hooded eyes

Em watched Rio trail his fingers along her sides to the tight muscles of her thighs. His head lowered to nibble his way from her breast to her belly button where he dipped his hot tongue and swirled through the indention. All the while he worked magic with his hands, massaging her muscles until she practically melted into the bed.

"Do you know how wonderful you are? Precious even?" Rio couldn't stop touching her despite his best intentions. The shock at seeing her in Purgatory still took him by surprise, even more so after the scene they'd just done. She'd taken to it like a fish to water, which wouldn't have surprised him if it wasn't his Emerson.

His Emerson. Like it or not that's how he'd thought of her for a long time now. Sure, she'd had an obvious crush on him as a teenager, and he'd grown protective over her because of it. But ever since she'd returned from college, it had been his turn to lust after her, and he'd felt guilty about it. Not only was there a pretty big age gap between them, there was the fact that as his best friend's sister that put her clearly in the do not touch *ever* category.

So much for that plan.

Lying next to her now, soothing her back to reality, his erection throbbed to be inside her. Something that wasn't about to go away.

"How are you now, Em, feeling better?"

"I felt fine before, I just needed some privacy to relax, but now I need—" She hesitated.

"You need what?" She didn't have to speak the words for him to know but he really wanted to hear her say it.

"I need you, Rio. I need you inside me. I need to know this is real."

"Oh, it's real all right." His fingers slid between her legs into her slick heat to find her hot and ready. She had no idea how bad his belly trembled with the desire to be buried inside her. To have her legs wrapped around him as she screamed in ecstasy when he made her come. His hand stilled. "If you don't want to go through with this, you need to tell me now. This changes everything and if we go any further, I don't think I could stop."

She tilted her hips in his hand so he cupped her sex. "I don't want you to stop." She stared back at him with determination and desire in her eyes. "I want you to take me."

Her words ignited the fuse that exploded his control. He grabbed her wrists and shoved them above her head, holding her there with one hand while his fingers rubbed at her clit until she whimpered next to him. He couldn't play anymore, couldn't wait another second to have her wet tightness sucking him inside.

He moved over her and gripped her wrists tighter, locking her into place, and crushed his mouth to hers. Her taste, smooth like a fine wine, drove him over the edge until his knee nudged her legs farther apart and his swollen tip hovered at her entrance.

Ripping his mouth from hers, he gazed down

at her flushed face. Those swollen ruby lips still beckoned, but he had to hear her say it one more time. "Tell me, Em, tell me again."

With no hesitation she looked at him and spoke. "Take me, please," she moaned.

The smooth, wet skin of her pussy teased him as he parted her folds with his shaft. Agony swept through him as he tried to go slow and not hurt her. She was a tiny thing.

"Hurry, Rio, I need more." Her pleading words did him in as he unleashed the force of his need and drove to his balls in one smooth thrust.

Rio drew back, leaving just the tip at her entrance before once again plunging deep. Emerson's legs squeezed his sides when her hips bucked upward. In and out he repeated, her nails digging into his arms and back on each thrust.

Harsh breathing blending with moans and grunts drove his passion and need to a frenzy.

Take me. Take me. He heard her command in his head over and over as her muscles tightened and his balls drew tight against his skin, tingling with the beginning of his release. She was forbidden and he'd taken her anyways, and now he needed more. Needed it all.

Her sex spasmed around him with her orgasm as she let loose a scream that filled the room, and likely the club. He withdrew once more as the powerful wave of lust and satisfaction surged over him and into her. Muscles rippled and shuddered as he continued to pump into her until replete, then he collapsed over her.

Their hearts beat together in a race to catch their breath as the implications of what they'd done crashed into him. He would definitely have some explaining to do. He didn't want to lose his best friend, but Em was important to him. He wanted her as his girlfriend, his submissive. Hell, probably more.

Realizing he was crushing her petite frame, he slipped from her body and rolled from the bed. Stepping into the nearby bathroom, he grabbed a soft cloth and soaked it in hot water, and returned to her.

Her gaze tracked him, careful and cautious. She looked nervous.

"Please don't tell me that you regret what happened." Her voice came out soft and anxious, maybe afraid.

He blew out a harsh breath and a hard sigh. "No, Em, not regret."

She sat up quickly and moved to the other side of the bed, dragging the sheet around her body since she had no clothes in the room.

"Where are you going?"

"I'm leaving before you break my heart." She stumbled in the bedding and he rushed the corner of the bed, blocking her exit.

"You're not leaving."

"Yes. I am. I saw your face, heard the resignation in the sigh. I know what comes next and I'd rather not hear it."

Tears leaked from her eyes and tore at his

heart. She'd misunderstood. "Not only are you not leaving tonight, if I have anything to say about it, you may never leave."

She stopped dead in her tracks, her head bowed to the floor. Seconds ticked by and she didn't move, only the sound of her breathing filled the room.

"Em, look at me." His fingers reached for her chin and tipped her head back so that her moist eyes were again visible to him. She really did look different without the mass of curls surrounding her face. She'd become quite the chameleon.

"Your brother may hurt me for this, but I'm not letting you go. That's if you'll still have me."

She hesitated for several minutes before a sly grin worked its way across her face. The sheet dropped and she jumped into his arms laughing and kissing at his neck and shoulders until they tumbled together on the bed.

"I'll take that as a yes."

"Are you crazy? Do you know how long I have waited for this day? Of course it's a yes."

Her nipples pressed against his chest and he couldn't resist reaching between them to tweak one of them. He wanted them in his mouth again, the tender tips between his teeth until she shrieked for him to stop. He was so going to enjoy testing her limits.

"You do realize this changes everything between us? I'm hard enough to live with as a friend, but as a Dom..."

"I've heard the stories." She pushed her

fingers through his hair. Fresh lust kicked him in the gut. The look on her face...

"Well, take what you've heard and multiply it by ten and maybe you'll hit the extent of what I have planned for you."

"Whatever you want, Rio," she whispered.

"Don't go making promises your butt can't cash sweetheart."

Rio locked his arms around her and flipped her over until she lay underneath him, belly down.

"But I'll take it as a start." Despite the amazing orgasm he'd just had, his cock began to stir. If he had his way, and he would, there would be many more even bigger orgasms through the rest of this night. Standing up, he rubbed the pearly cheeks of her ass before letting one of his hands fall with a good hard smack.

She gasped and swiveled her head. "What was that for?"

A wicked grin spread across his face. "I think it's time for your next lesson."

Whipped

Chapter One

The slap of leather against naked flesh echoed in Walker's brain, tormenting his need, which was already at a feverish level. He stepped, mindless, from the club into the harsh, biting wind. A few die-hard smokers huddled close to the wall, the glowing embers of their addiction lighting the darkened patio. He wasn't a smoker, but it was the only place outside to catch his breath and maybe relocate the section of his brain where his control was stored.

He'd spent the last hour at the flogging station with Dex, watching and waiting—for what, he wasn't sure. There had been a steady stream of beautiful women in line waiting to get flogged by the most popular Dom in the club, but when the cadence of blows began to beat in rhythm with the pulse in his stiff dick he decided it was time to get some fresh air.

"Hey man, you gotta light?" One of the half naked, leather and black nail polish goth guys ambled over to him.

"No, don't smoke." And he wanted to be left

alone.

Goth Boy gave him a confused look before he turned and wandered back to his group.

What am I doing here?

He'd moved to town six months ago after a long and difficult break up. By chance he'd overhead some clients talking about Purgatory and, his curiosity piqued, he'd come to check it out. It had been everything he'd expected, plus so much more. The club seemed to cater to a variety of clientele from the straight goth crowd to the extreme fetishists, and the place was definitely a playground for the voyeur. Drawn to the upstairs VIP area and its many play stations, he came here as often as he could get away.

Lately, though, simply observing wasn't enough, and the few times Dex had handed him the flogger to take over when he needed a break had been very nice. What he craved, although, ran much deeper than flogging a stranger. There were willing and available submissives in the club he could play with, but he yearned for a connection and a level of submission he doubted most women here would understand. Besides, he hated the word play, and the first time it came out of a sub's mouth he was usually gone.

Walker pulled his collar around his neck and shivered in the cold. He couldn't stay out here much longer, so it was either go back inside or head on home. At least now his body was under a semblance of control. A glance at his watch showed ten-thirty, still early for a Saturday night.

Fine. He'd go in and watch a few of the stations, chat with Dex, then head on home.

Alone. Again.

Walker pulled the heavy door open and hustled inside, seeking the awaiting heat and excitement. Bonnie, the door supervisor, smiled at him, and he returned a warm greeting.

"Walker, Sir, I can't believe you're out there without a jacket."

He'd chatted with her many times and found her as genuine as they came.

"I'd tell you again to just call me Walker, but you aren't ever going to do it are you?" She'd lost her Dom last year to cancer, and while she seemed to be embracing life once again she'd firmly stood against finding another man.

She blushed and lowered her gaze. "No, Sir."

He understood her grief and knew that one day someone worthy would come along and get her back on her knees where she so loved to be.

"No worries, Bonnie, I can see what a good girl you are and would certainly never hold that against you. No one should." He touched her chin and tilted her head until their gazes met. "It is chilly outside, so be sure to bundle up before you go home tonight." He liked the fact that he was getting to know everyone here and making friends. It never hurt to be around like-minded people who accepted him as is with no judgment.

A slow smile spread across her face and she

nodded before turning her attention to the customer who'd come through the door behind him.

Glancing down on the main floor, he saw the rope swing in motion with Leo astride his latest victim as they swung from one end of the room to the other. The crowd went wild as the pretty blonde's face bloomed in ecstasy at the attention.

The club was in full Saturday night swing as he moved slowly through the crowds around each play station. He couldn't even get close enough to the extreme booth to see what they were currently offering up, so he turned and set off in the direction of the flogging stations.

By now his friend would be looking to take a break, but Walker wasn't sure he was up to wielding anymore tonight. Already his groin ached enough to give him second thoughts to any offers he might receive. He could use a good dick sucking right about now.

Kat and Cindi were busy marking the hell out of a couple of subbie boys when he walked up. Their arms arched back and sprang forward with as much force as they could find. The whoosh of the air splitting for the dozens of knotted tails caught and held his attention as they connected with bare, red streaked skin.

Dex stood next to him, watching and enjoying the show those ladies loved to put on. Every male subbie in the room ate it up and no doubt wished it was them like it was nobody's business.

"They've got some real pain sluts in the booth tonight," Dex mumbled.

"That's for sure. A little different from what you've got going on, huh?"

"Wait until you meet my next appointment, Cass. She's—"

"She's what?" A sultry sexy voice sounded behind them and both men jerked around to see.

"Why, she's the most beautiful woman in the room, that's what."

"Nice save, Dex," she murmured.

Walker stood speechless at the sight before him. Long, raven dark hair framed a narrow face, and dark eyes surrounded by thick inky lashes that watched him curiously. Her nose was ordinary but the red lips underneath drew him like a moth to flame. He lingered there watching them part slightly while her tongue darted to the edge. He felt his cock stir in his pants as his own curiosity piqued.

"Cass, here for another session, I see? Do you need to feel my flogger on your skin?" Dex teased her until she broke the look between them to turn to his friend.

"Need is overrated these days, Dex, you know that. But I can't deny I do enjoy coming to see you on occasion. Even a girl like me enjoys a little fun now and then."

Dex snorted and shook his head.

Walker closed his eyes and let her smoky voice float over him. There was more to what she said, he could sense it. The slight hitch in between sentences, the nervous way she moved her hands, all combined to make him curious to know who this Cass was and the story behind her.

"Well come on, sugar, you're in luck. You're next on my list." He led her to his station and waited for her to get in place.

A sexy ass swayed in a tight, low-slung denim skirt when she moved. Her outfit was a far cry from the leather and PVC wear of many in the crowd, but somehow the simplicity of denim riding low on her hips and a crisp, white cotton half-shirt leaving her midriff bare did more for him than all the big tits with their nipples covered by tiny strips of electrical tape. No, he was an ass man through and through, and the more she twitched it the more he thought about fucking it.

She had the art of teasing down to a fine science, and obviously she and Dex played this game regularly. He, however, was not a man to toy with unless you were fully prepared to follow through. He was more worked up than he had a right to be, but that didn't change the fact his body had come to life the moment he'd heard her voice.

Walker watched her. Slender fingers lifted to the buttons of her blouse and made quick time easing them each free. His heart raced with no other explanation than excitement at something or someone new. With her hands gripping the edges of the shirt, her head tilted up and her gaze connected with his.

He easily recognized the uncertainty in her eyes as well as the caution she directed at him, but underneath those surface reactions he saw the hunger. Gut deep, aching need crying out for relief. That very look would be what he thought of later tonight when he was jacking off again.

"Did you all of a sudden develop a case of shyness, Cass?" Dex winked at her and smiled.

"Don't be silly, I'm just enjoying the moment." Her eyes cleared in a split second.

"Uh huh."

She turned and faced the large St. Andrew's Cross filling Dex's space and jerked her shirt from her shoulders. More creamy skin and a flash of a white lace bra cupping high breasts filled his view for a few seconds before she settled her front against the smooth wood of the cross.

Besides the slim straps of her bra and the small skirt, Cass stood naked with her arms stretched above her along the lines of the wood. Walker stared, mesmerized by the expanse of tanned skin peeking from underneath the long fall of hair that touched the tip of a tribal tattoo on her lower back. Someone else might look at her mark and refer to it as her tramp stamp, but to him it seemed sexy, even sensual.

Dex whispered at her ear, low enough so only she heard as his hands deftly buckled her wrist into the leather cuff at the top. A moan sounded from her at whatever he said and her hips wiggled against the wood. This was going to be very interesting.

Dex glanced at him as he walked to her other side, revealing a heat that surprised him. Of all the floggers in the club he always remained cool and detached. Until now.

Dex stepped close, closer than necessary to get to her other hand and Walker couldn't miss the bulge in his pants as he did. A swift desire to pull him away from her and take over welled deep in his gut. Why he suddenly wanted to protect her made no sense. Dex was the best in the club and would care for her better than any Dom he'd ever seen. Still, his fists clenched tight at his side to keep from grabbing him and hauling him away.

"Walker, you okay?"

"Yeah." Except for the desire to wipe the knowing grin from his friend's face.

"I've never seen Cass react like that before I've even started. She holds onto that control of hers with an iron fist."

"Why is that?"

"There's a history there she doesn't want anyone to know. About six months ago she started coming in twice a month like clockwork. She's always friendly and eager, but it's not hard to see that she holds back."

"Interesting."

"It is, isn't it?" Dex had turned back to Cass as his question faded into their surroundings.

While he went to pick the right flogger, Walker moved to the side of the booth so if Cass turned her head he would see her face. He wanted to watch her reactions. Already her breathing appeared slightly labored as she anticipated the session. Every few breaths she took her body trembled, causing his to tighten further until he was as strung out as she.

He wanted her and, unless he missed his guess, which he rarely did when it came to reading people, so did Dex.

The session began with a simple suede flogger consisting of a multitude of long tails and various knots that Dex used to trail across her arms and back until a soft "please" fell from her lips. A sign the little sub was getting desperate for more.

He wanted to be the one coaxing the pleasure from Cass, but it would be awkward, to say the least, to ask for permission to do so. So instead he remained on the sidelines, rigid with need and longing for a woman who wouldn't even be described as pretty by others, but to him had become the most sensual creature he'd seen in a very long time.

"I know, baby. It's coming."

Dex talked to her in hushed tones that no one besides the three of them could have heard. As he raised his arm and delivered the tails across her back in a sharp blow, the sounds and people around them faded away. All of the focus was on Cass and her pleasure, fulfilling the need she'd come to Purgatory for.

Wrists twisted and turned so the tails moved in a sideways figure eight, and light pink marks began to appear across the skin of her back.

Even while watching the flogging from the corner of his eyes Walker didn't take his gaze from the profile of her face. He willed her to turn and look at him, desperate to see her every reaction to his friend's superior skills.

As the falls to her backside increased, her hands clenched and unclenched into tights fists as she automatically pulled against her bindings. She'd been given a safe word to use if at any time the flogging became too much for her, but based on her body language she wouldn't be using it anytime soon.

Walker glanced at Dex to see his friend lost in concentration, his hand flipping the flogger both expertly and automatically as he watched for any sign of distress or pleasure on her part. On a loud moan from Cass, Dex looked over with a shit-eating grin stamped on his face. The man took pride in his ability to mold every submissive in his care to the perfect writhing ball of pleasure.

When Walker turned back to Cass, he caught her staring at him. Their gazes met and held and her lips parted, a moan rolling out and over him. His stomach seized as the need emanating from her melded with his, driving them both to the precipice of no return. With little thought to their surroundings his palm rubbed over his dick, pushing the seam of his pants into the sensitive skin. If she kept looking at him like that he was going to come in his fucking pants like a horny teenager.

Energy buzzed through his veins, as his

innate need to be in control fought for dominance over the situation. He had to fight the urge to snatch the flogger from Dex and whip her until she begged to come for him.

Dex halted his movements and moved to the wall obviously looking to make a switch. Her pleas to not stop tore at his resistance as he took another step toward the platform. Dex chuckled from the other side, probably amused by his behavior but Walker was far beyond caring what anyone though of him at the moment.

This woman had managed to drag him in and pull him out of the shell he'd been waiting in. He'd decided actively looking was a waste of his time and other than his minor activities here at the club he'd buried his need for more.

Until tonight, when he'd seen her.

Tears rolled down her cheek as she watched him, her hips pressing into the cross. She was so close to her orgasm she'd resorted to rubbing that clit of hers against the edge of the wood in a desperate attempt to finish what Dex had started.

"If you come before he's finished, I'll make sure you're punished." The harsh command tumbled from Walker's mouth before his brain even considered them. He had no rights here, yet he couldn't help himself, he had to take charge.

Her sobs halted and her eyes widened in surprise. Seconds stretched out as she stared at him and he waited for the sassy retort he knew lingered on her tongue. Dex had returned to his place behind her and waited as well. He'd obviously overhead his statement and hesitated giving her a chance to respond.

On a long exhale she finally spoke. "Yes, Sir."

The tightness in his chest released, as did the breath he hadn't realized he'd been holding. He nodded to Dex, who stepped closer this time with two new floggers. With the flick of both wrists the leather tails wrapped around her thighs, under her skirt and perilously close to her cunt. He'd not struck hard but it'd been unexpected, and the wild look in her eyes pleased him.

"Tell him," Walker ordered. This time she didn't hesitate.

"More please, Dex. I need more." Her whispered voice hitched when she spoke.

He didn't take his eyes off of her as Dex increased the tempo of leather slapping against flesh and denim as he covered every inch, from her calves to the bare shoulders he itched to soothe.

Dex got back into the zone and Cass trembled and moaned with every touch. The sound of her arousal neared peak as her hips jerked forward, looking for anything to rub in her desperate attempt to increase the friction against her clit.

Walker not only wanted to bring her to the edge himself, he wanted to hold her there a little longer. With her chained to his wall without clothes, he could test and tease her until she exploded from overload. Everything inside told him she would respond to his brand of control, even thrive under it.

"Walker." Dex's voice broke into his thoughts, forcing his focus on this scene not the future. The subtle nod from his friend was all the encouragement he needed.

Walker moved, eating up the little distance left between Cass and himself. With his head bent and his lips close to her ear, heat rose from her skin, drawing him in.

"Cass, I know what you need. You want someone to direct, to give their permission, to allow you to come. But I'm not inclined to give it unless you ask for it." In reality he didn't care if she begged this time. He wanted to watch her come from the flogging, with little else for stimulation.

"Please." The words trembled from her mouth. "I have to come."

He begged to differ, but she obviously had a plan and they didn't know each other at all— except in the way that like always knows like, and this little sub had a deep dark need she was afraid of. The least he could do was not get in her way of satisfaction. Which, of course, had nothing to do with him wanting to see her writhing in ecstasy in front of the crowd.

He glanced at Dex, who delivered the final strike to her sides, the long leather tails wrapping around her inner thighs and delivering a swift pop against her clit. The nub he now imagined swollen and hard, waiting for

Eliza Gayle

the attention it deserved.

A long scream, drowned out by the throbbing industrial music, tore from her mouth. Her head fell back, her hair shaking loose and her hands yanking frantically on the bonds that held her in place.

Walker couldn't keep his hands off of her. His fingers settled on her waist, her muscles clenching underneath as she rode the wave of pleasure Dex—and maybe he in some small part—had created for her. Silky strands of hair brushed against his burning skin like a gentle wave of water on a hot day.

God, he wanted to tear off her panties, bury his head between her legs, and lap up every bit of cream she spilled. She'd be so fucking wet and hot, his dick jerked with the thought of it. If she thought this climax was good, he'd show her much better with his tongue.

As she came back down, he listened to the harsh breaths in and out of her lungs. Little aftershocks rippled across her body while Dex unfastened one arm and then reached for the other. With her wrists loose, she began to slump, and Walker scooped her into his arms and carried her to the sofa in the corner.

He cradled her to his chest, allowing her the time she needed to recover as well the time he needed to get his body and mind back under control. She was not his. Hell, he didn't even know her. Yet the intoxicating scent of vanilla mixed with her sexual musk seared into his brain, never to be forgotten.

She stirred in his lap, her eyes fluttering but not opening. Her skin glistened with a gentle pink flush, lips slightly parted as her breathing slowed to normal.

"Stop staring at me, you're making me uncomfortable," she whispered.

"I can't help it. I'm not sure I've ever seen anything so delectable."

Her eyes popped open—pools of ocean blue stared up at him, a look so intense yet laced with sorrow. She twisted away from his chest, her feet moving to the floor.

"You don't have to lie to me, it's unnecessary. I'm not a fool, you know." She rushed to her things and redressed quickly.

Anger radiated from her as the soft submissive look disappeared, the mask of a woman unaffected replacing it. Taken aback by her outburst, he said nothing, unsure what had happened.

Staring daggers at him, she spoke to Dex. "As always, Dex, you are the master of Purgatory. Thank you."

The last two words were spoken softly and without sarcasm before she turned on her heels and rushed into the crowd of the club. Walker warred with himself on whether to go after her or not. Everything about her screamed his, even the temper. Yet, right now she needed space. Time to recover. He'd have preferred in his arms, but there would be a next time he was certain.

"What the hell was that all about?" Walker

turned to face his friend in time to see the mocking smile plastered across his features.

"The funniest thing I've seen in a long time, I'd say." Dex shook his head and picked up his cleaning spray and towel and proceeded to begin the wipe down of the cross before the next in line came for their turn.

"This is not funny, Dex. That woman is amazing, but she's in no condition to be wandering around by herself." He tried to catch a glimpse of her through the people crowded together but she'd disappeared from sight.

Dex turned back, his eyes narrowed. "Cass is a complicated woman, Walker. As a submissive she's had her heart torn out."

"What happened?" He'd better hear the story sooner rather than later so he knew what he was dealing with.

Dex's shoulders sagged as he finished cleaning up and hung the floggers on their hooks. His reluctance to continue did little to dissuade him as he waited for an answer. Time passed and Cass got farther away, possibly even gone for the night. He would have to rely on Dex to fill him in.

"There's something about her, Dex. Something that reached out to me like nothing has in a really long time." He was taking a chance on revealing his own secrets to his friend, but if he wanted information then he'd do what he had to in order for him to understand.

"I'm not blind, I saw how you reacted to her

and how she reacted to you as well. I've been doing this a damn long time and thousands of submissives have passed through here with every story you could think of and then some." He picked up the clipboard and consulted the sign ups before he dropped it back on the small table. "Cass has been coming in for months and it's taken a while to get even half her story, and most of that from rumors around the club not from the woman herself."

Walker nodded. He liked that Cass had not been an easy read or willing to open up to any Dom who would listen. He had so many questions for Dex, but he knew him well enough to know that he needed to be patient. He would reveal what he wanted to when he was good and ready.

"From what I understand, she lived as a twenty-four-seven slave for some time until about a year ago when her Dom up and disappeared. As in packed up and left town without a word, leaving her to find out when she returned to an empty house one day after work."

Walker rubbed at his chest, annoyance already pressing down on him.

"Why?"

"No idea. For that answer you'd have to ask the lady herself, and so far I haven't been given an opening into her life for even the first personal question." Dex's fingers absently stroked the tails of his favored suede flogger as he spoke. "I think she's been trying to withdraw from the lifestyle for a while now, but every few weeks she shows up for a flogging, desperation written all over her face despite that pretty smile she fools everyone with."

Walker nodded in understanding. He and Dex were more alike than he'd thought. They'd both seen through the wall she'd built up to protect herself.

"A fucking shame if you ask me. Her need is palpable when she walks into the room. She's afraid to even try to open up to anyone, but that fear will never erase what her soul clamors for."

"You want her?" Walker didn't really need to ask the question but he felt obligated. The more Dex told him the more he wanted to go after her.

"I feel protective of her."

Walker nodded. He could read between the lines. Dex did have a thing for Cass, but not enough to pursue or push it. Which left him open to take her for himself. Now he just had to convince Cass she didn't need to run away.

"I'm going to see if I can find her. Make sure she's okay."

"Uh huh. She's probably gone. Cass isn't one for socializing around here. She has a need, gets it filled as best she can, and then goes back to her life to pretend everything will be fine.

"And where is that life?"

Dex shrugged. "No one knows, or at least no one says. There are people in the lifestyle who make it a point to know everything about everyone, but they also guard that information."

A pretty young girl arrived at the station, eager anticipation written on her face.

"Unfortunately, Walker, you're on your own with this one." With that his friend moved over to his next victim and led her to his cross.

Chapter Two

Walker surveyed the crowd as he moved through the club. As it grew later, the place filled to capacity making it difficult to find anyone. It was like looking for a needle in a haystack. At the exit he decided he'd head out and come back tomorrow. Eventually she'd return–over the years he'd learned to be patient to achieve what he wanted. He jerked his coat tight and pulled open the door.

In the parking lot, a few partiers rushed to their vehicles, something Walker did as well. With key in hand, he contemplated how long it would take him to get in and get the car warm.

"Fuck!"

Walker whirled at the feminine voice to find the object of his desire, pacing the alley behind the club. A smile tugged at the corner of his mouth. So she'd not left after all. Good or bad, he would take it as a positive sign. Although, her being out here alone in the dark seemed irresponsible, to say the least.

Forgetting the cold and his car, he headed

toward the woman moving back and forth oblivious to those around her.

"Cass?"

She whirled on him, her arms coming up to guard her body. "Jesus Christ, don't sneak up on someone like that."

"What are you doing out here, are you all right?" He doubted she would tell him if she weren't.

Her shoulders eased an inch or two. "I'm fine. I needed some fresh air and time to think."

"Probably not the safest place for thinking." He couldn't not say it. She wasn't thinking with a clear head. Not after the whipping Dex had given her. She may have snapped out of it pretty quickly, but there was a crash coming sooner or later.

"Please don't presume to know what's best for me." She stopped moving to glare at him. "I may not fully understand why I reacted to you the way I did, but I do know how to take care of myself."

He edged forward, needing to get closer to this woman who drew him no matter what she said. Any other man probably would have left before she could utter another word. All they would see were complications, he saw a challenge.

Her head dropped forward, her gaze staring toward the ground. "I can take care of myself."

"Yes, you've said that." Another step and he'd be close enough to feel her body heat. "Why don't we go somewhere and get a cup of coffee, we can talk about it."

Her head jerked up, a wild look in her eyes.

"You can't say that to me!" The panic welled in her voice.

Walker raised his hands in surrender. "Okay no coffee then."

"No, not that." Moisture pooled in her eyes. "You can't tell a woman like me that she is the most delectable thing you've ever seen. It's just not right."

"Why the hell not?"

"Because it's bullshit and we both know it."

Now he was getting mad. What the fuck?

He grabbed her around the waist and hauled her against him. "Let's get something straight right now. I never, and I mean never, say something I don't mean. Life is too fucking short to pretend to be something you're not or to blow smoke up someone's ass with a lie or a half-truth. So if I tell you something you can damn well count on me meaning every word."

"But—but—"

The confused look in her eyes did him in. Whatever idiot had left her had shaken her confidence. Something he never wanted to see in a submissive, but the fight in her gave him hope.

"You were perfect tonight. It took every ounce of my restraint not to pull you down and bend you over the bench and have my way. Which would have been balls deep inside you with your pussy clenching around me in ecstasy."

Her breath hitched, a strangled little moan coming out. A sexy sound that pulled at his gut and stroked over his balls. Her eyes blazed hot when he threaded his fingers through her hair and tilted her back so her throat and neck were open to him. The rich black strands brushed his hand like the finest silk and even in the dim light of the alley he watched her gaze darken with more than a hint of arousal.

She turned him on in ways he hadn't been in a long time. His lustful imagination ran wild as he envisioned her in his personal dungeon, naked and ready to serve with that very look in her eyes. Desire and desperation.

Unable to resist, he pressed his lips to her shoulder, opening his mouth to allow his teeth to scrape against the flesh. When the heat of his tongue licked across her skin, she jerked into his arms. God, she tasted so fucking good.

He nipped at her neck, absorbing the vibration of her low moan.

"Please," she whispered.

Logical thought began to evaporate as he pushed his thigh between her legs, forcing her to spread for him. God help him, he wanted to see her come again and he couldn't wait. Her hips tilted to meet his moves, pushing the mound of her sex against him. She didn't act like a woman afraid or one who wanted him to stop. No, her fingers dug into his jacket so hard, he was certain had it not been for the thick layers, she'd be shredding his skin.

He sucked at her flesh until red streaks appeared, marking her as his. She might carry the welts from her flogging by another man, but these spots she'd see every time she glanced in a mirror for the next couple of days and remember whose mouth had taken possession.

"You should've gone home, Cass."

Her head shook violently. "No, this—please I need this."

Walker covered her lips, stroking his tongue into the eager cavern. The exotic taste of a woman in need exploded in his head. Her tongue met his as they curled together, tormenting him with her easy acceptance of his every move. He wanted to gentle his actions, not go too fast and scare her away. There would be time to explore the darker side of things when they knew each other better.

Then she bit him.

Walker reared his head back without loosening his grip on her hair. Her eyes shone like twin pools of molten lava and, unless he missed his mark, a mocking dare sparkled there as well. His control snapped and his hand jerked her head back, his free hand wrapping around her slender neck. With little thought to anything but conquering the woman in his arms, his lips slammed over hers.

Every one of his brain cells fried together to burn him alive. Hips bucked, pressing leather against silk, rubbing his dick across her clit. He wanted her bad, to the point his groin and balls ached with it. Her hands scraped at his thigh before he felt them move to lift her skirt, giving him access to the soft cushion of her pussy underneath. He needed to stop. This was no place for lust, especially the out of control variety.

The knowledge anyone could turn the corner and catch them did little to dissuade him with the warm moisture of her flooded cunt soaking onto his pants. Tempting him. Torturing him.

"Oh, God, Walker! More. Please. Please. Don't. stop." Her cries washed over him, tugging hard at what shred of self-control he still had.

"Not here. Not like this." She deserved so much more.

"Please. I need you now." Her cry broke on a choked sob.

Moving his hips to give him space, he slipped his hand from her throat to the edge of her panties. Cass shivered under his hands as fingers found her bare shaven slit and the coating of moisture slickening her skin.

On a groan he sank into the blazing heat of her pussy and swirled through her juices before pushing a single finger inside her. Tight, clenching flesh squeezed around him, shredding any objection he might have mustered.

"Oh, God!" she gasped, her hands grasping at his shoulders.

"You're so damned wet." He stilled inside her and pressed his forehead to hers. He could do this. Give her what she needed and walk away. Save the rest for another day. If only her muscles would quit clenching around his finger, coating it with her juices.

"Please don't leave me like this. I can't take it." Her hips moved drawing him farther inside her. "Please don't leave."

The simple plea in her voice echoed with a need that ripped the fight from his soul. They'd both walked a thin line back in the club and now, here in a dark alley, he'd broken every rule he had. For a woman he didn't even know.

A glimpse at her face found her eyes tightly closed. "Look at me, Cass." When she ignored his demand, he tugged at her hair, forcing her head back until she opened to him. Stark, naked hunger shone back at him.

"I know what you need, and I'm inclined to give it to you." He bent and scraped his teeth along her jaw while his finger stroked her, a gentle rubbing against sensitive tissues. "But you should consider that it won't end there. When your cream covers my hand, I'm going to fuck you right here, right now, and not care who might see you."

Her eyes rolled back in her head on a long, low moan.

"Is that what you want?"

Her tongue darted out to lick at her lips as she nodded furiously.

"Not good enough, little girl. If you can't say it, you certainly can't have it."

A shudder wracked her body as she looked at him. He knew the words hovered on her lips and he held his breath praying she would say them. Because if she walked away now, he didn't know how he could handle it.

Her reservations or fears would do little to deter him. He would take them as a challenge and break down the barriers she had built around her until they both burned in the lust arcing between them.

Waiting for her answer, he slid a second finger along the first, stretching her as he fucked into her. Either way he would feel her coming apart in his arms.

"Walker, you know I want this. More than want, I'm burning, aching."

On her admission he let his thumb graze over the hardened bud of her clit, applying just enough pressure to have her bucking against him.

"Take me. I can't stand it," she panted.

Patience gone, his hand jerked from her suckling flesh as he pushed her a few inches to the wall. He ripped at the waistband of his pants and shoved them open enough to free his cock and place it at the heated entrance of her pussy.

"This won't be gentle or nice." He warned when the first thrust buried him half inside her.

"Fuck gentle." She gasped.

He'd tried to prepare her with his fingers, but she was still so damned tight. The slightest movement sent pleasure shooting up his spine. He grabbed her leg and brought it around his waist opening her to take him fully. His hips pulled back, sliding his shaft slowly from the tight grip she had on him.

Eliza Gayle

"More?" He really did want to draw out the pleasure but this wasn't going to last long.

"Yes, yes," she whispered, her silky breath teasing his neck.

He plunged into her, parting tight muscles and soft flesh with the aid of her slick juices coating him.

She cried out, a guttural sound of pleasure and ecstasy that ripped at his balls and any control he'd managed to retain.

"Walker..."

"I know, baby, I've got you and I'm not letting go."

She screamed into his neck as he drew back, dragging over sensitive nerve endings, eliciting his own groan.

Before she could breathe again he drove inside her. There couldn't be any more stopping as his thrusts continued over and over— stroking, forging, impaling, claiming the woman in his arms as she fractured in orgasm. He drew out her pleasure with half a dozen more plunges until his balls ached and the pressure became too much. On a rough grunt he buried his head in her shoulders as the fierce jets of release shook him to the bone.

He wrapped his arm around her and pulled her off the wall and tighter in his arms. He wanted to talk. To say something important, like how exquisite she was, but he couldn't. He was no stranger to urgent lust or quickie fucks, but it was the first time someone had blown his mind. How do you tell a stranger you can't let her go? That in one night he'd found the submissive, no, the woman he didn't even know he was searching for?

Chapter Three

Walker released Cass slowly, making sure she could stand before he stepped back. Immediately cool air flowed between them and the stark reality of a parking lot came into sharp focus as they put themselves back together.

"We need to go somewhere private, discuss what's happening." He held out his hand, expecting her to take his lead.

Her head shook furiously as her eyes remained looking down at her clothes. "No, I need to go home."

"Did I hurt you?" He didn't want her pulling away now. He wanted to hear about her life, learn what made her tick all the time. He couldn't stop now.

"Oh, God no. That was more incredible than anything I expected."

He cringed. He could hear the kiss off coming a mile away.

"I have to get home, I have work early."

"At least let me make sure you get home

okay."

Her head jerked again, but not before he saw the wet drops clinging to her lashes.

"No, really, I'm fine and I don't even live that far away." She fumbled in her pocket and pulled out a key—to her car, he presumed.

Walker hid his smile when she straightened her spine and fingered her hair into some form of normalcy before looking at him again.

"I want to see you again." He didn't know what else to say, he was quickly losing control of the situation and she didn't look about to budge on anything.

"It's okay, Walker. I'm fine. You don't have to worry about me, say things you don't want to or anything really."

He snagged her by the wrist, catching her off guard, and hauled her closer to him. "I thought we already settled that I never do or say things I don't mean. Do we need to go over that again?"

Her head shook but she remained quiet.

This close he smelled the sex on her. Both his and her scents mixed were a heady thing. Amazingly his cock stirred again at the mere thought of being inside of her.

"Good." He dug into his wallet and pulled out a card. "Here's my card. Call me when you get home and we'll figure something out." He didn't leave it as a question. She needed to know he expected to hear from her. "Okay?"

"Yes, Sir," she whispered.

Unable to avoid her already kiss swollen lips, he slanted his mouth over hers. The now familiar taste of her spiked through him sending shards of renewed lust along his spine. There was so much he wanted to do with her, alone. Talk, touch every naked inch of her lush body, watch her ass bloom as he spanked it right before he took her there. The image of her shaking, gasping for air the entire time, would be what he thought of until he saw her again.

Despite her talk of urgency to get home, the hunger he tasted in her kiss and the heat emanating from her told him a completely different story. It might kill him tonight to let her go but he would, he had to. She obviously needed some time to think through her fears.

She would leave tonight with the knowledge that he was an understanding man, a Dom she could trust to put her needs first.

As her lips moved under his, her tongue curling around his, he tried to understand what made her so different from all the others. Why did he want to take her home and cherish her, taking care of every need she'd ever suffered as unfulfilled?

When her teeth nipped at his lower lip, he twisted his hand in her hair, rubbing the soft strands against his skin. He no longer cared about the why when his cock rose in strength once again. He forced himself from her mouth.

"If you're serious about going, you'd better go now." If she didn't walk now he wasn't sure he'd let her go. A frightening thought, but the wicked need lancing through him was the only warning he had.

She nodded and walked away without another word. He doubted either one of them could have said anything more.

Chapter Four

Two weeks later and Walker still hadn't seen Cass—or, as he affectionately referred to her now, his little brat—again. When her call had finally come several days after their encounter, he'd been about to go out of his mind with not hearing from her. He should have known better than to leave their future communication up to her.

He recalled the sweet hesitation in her voice, soothing his anger and worry.

"I—I'm sorry I haven't called."

"Are you okay?"

"Yes."

The fast response came out forced and awkward. Skittish even. The same vulnerability that had him fucking her in a parking lot gripped him by the balls yet again.

"You should be paddled."

She didn't respond, but he didn't miss the catch in her breath at his words. "In fact, we need to get together and discuss whatever this is that's going on."

"Things went too far."

Fuck. He didn't want it to end like this. "Do you regret that?"

"Not exactly. No regrets—it's just—I don't know."

He'd broken every one of his rules that night. No sex on the first night of meeting a potential submissive was right up there with always using a safe word.

"Tell me."

"I'm not ready."

He'd wanted to call bullshit right then but decided instead to give her the space she thought she needed.

Until now. He'd waited long enough.

He pulled his car into a parking spot at the edge of the lot and smoothly stepped outside. He and Cass had talked several times, taking some time to get to know each other.

He'd tried to coax what pained her the most out of her but she'd remained pretty tight lipped, instead spending most of her time talking about her small specialty wine and coffee shop business in the art district, Grape and Bean.

As a slave to his neighborhood Starbucks, he'd never been in her place, but he drove by here every day on his way to work. The white cottage frame building had a large covered patio out front with wrought iron furniture and colorful plants. Creating an inviting place for customers to linger was a smart business move. He looked forward to seeing her in this environment—the strong woman running a successful business in contrast to the sexy submissive he'd fucked outside a sex club.

He strode through the door, chimes announcing his arrival, to find a line ten feet deep at the coffee counter. Three employees rushed around filling orders, but his brat was nowhere in sight. He knew she would be here since she'd told him how busy her Saturdays were. Another reason she'd come up with for not seeing him again.

"What can I get you?"

The question shook him from his thoughts as a pretty Asian girl took his order. Straight black coffee in hand, he found a small booth in the corner and settled in. He'd cleared his schedule for the entire day and night with his only goal to talk to Cass in person. She needed to face him, face what happened between them and decide if she could give in to the need he knew slowly ate at her.

There were times when the conversations turned serious and sexy that he heard it in her voice. She'd make a breathless sound that had his cock straining against his pants and had him masturbating more often than usual. Not like it was doing any good, though. No, satisfaction for them both would come together as they explored their budding relationship.

The door behind the counter swung open and Cass walked through, and while he'd recognize her anywhere she looked far different from the woman two weeks ago. Gone were the sexy, skin tight clothes, replaced with conservative khakis and a pretty pink blouse that hid what he knew to be the sexiest damn curves he'd seen in a long time.

Her hair was pinned into a neat bun with a few wisps of escaped dark hair curling loosely around her face. A sharp spear of arousal punched through his gut at the sensual curve of her exposed neck. The memory of licking and biting her as clear as when she'd been wrapped in his arms, riding his cock for all she was worth.

Thank God for the table where he sat. She might not appreciate the sight of his dick tenting his pants as he watched her move around behind the counter, smiling and talking to customers and employees alike.

And what a smile. Broad and charming, lighting up her face with irresistible allure. How she couldn't see what that kind of beauty would do to a man amazed him. It wasn't always about big tits and blonde hair or a perfect body and skinny thighs. In the long run what radiated from the inside made for an enduring relationship.

He sipped at his cooling drink, waiting. Observing her at work could be as enlightening as some of their phone chats had been. She donned a small purple apron emblazoned with the Grape and Bean logo, grabbed a rag and headed his way, probably to clean up the abandoned tables now that the crowd had thinned considerably.

He admired the shape of her bare arm as she wiped a table down, a visible line of muscle flexing under taut and tanned skin. She'd mentioned her addiction to running on the local greenways at least three times a week and he imagined it served as an outlet for emotions as much as it did for keeping in shape.

As she moved closer and closer to where he sat his muscles tightened, bracing for the reaction he expected. While she cleaned the table next to his her gaze slid toward him and she froze in place when recognition dawned.

He focused on her face. The almost imperceptible tightening around her mouth, the alarm clearly shining in her eyes. She wore a hint of makeup that served to add, not detract from, the mask of innocence she carried here. No one would ever guess the darkness that laid in wait inside her, begging for freedom.

"Cass." He nearly winced at the harsh, gravelly sound of his voice.

"Walker."

He'd managed to knock her off balance by showing up unannounced, a fact that he liked very much. She had barriers he wanted through, and not giving her time to prepare what to say served him well.

Although seeing her at all made him want to grab her by the hand and take her somewhere private, force her to confront him on the most basic level a woman could with a man.

"This is unexpected."

Although she tried to hide it, he caught the

subtle hesitation in her voice. The only outward indication that he'd rattled her at all.

"We need to talk."

"I don't have a lot of time right now," she insisted.

He looked around the shop, making a point to notice every customer who lingered. There were only three left and her employees had them all covered.

"Do what you need to do and I'll wait. When you have five minutes, come and join me. Then I'll get out of your hair."

Wariness turned to fear as she had to realize how serious he was. He didn't mind waiting at all but he'd say what he'd come to say before he left.

Her weight shifted from foot to foot a few times as he imagined her mind working through her options. He doubted she'd guess his intentions, but before the night was over, he would either possess the woman in front of him or watch her walk away for good.

"Fine," she sighed, slipping into the booth across from him. "I have five minutes now, but really you didn't have to come here for this. I would have been fine to hear it over the phone."

He opened his mouth to ask what she meant, but if his suspicions were right and she said them aloud he couldn't promise he wouldn't drag her over his knee right here in her place of business. Something he was sure she wouldn't easily forgive.

"Don't presume to think you know what I

have to say, my little brat." His voice carried humor in his statement, but he reinforced it with just enough steel for her to know how serious he was.

Her head bowed slightly and her eyes darted downward. The ease in which she expressed her submissiveness to him still amazed him. Rumors at the club had given him an impression of her experience, but it was times like these when none of that mattered and only what she felt in her heart did he want to see.

"That's better." He lowered his voice so no one nearby would accidentally overhear. "You've avoided seeing me for weeks and it had to stop."

"But—"

Walker raised his hand a few inches to stop her before she got started with her reasonable but tired excuses.

"Yes, I know how busy you are and I respect that. But I'm not stupid and I know you're avoiding me." He picked up her hand from the table and brushed his fingers across her knuckles, loving the shiver that coursed through her at his touch. "I need you, Cass. That one night at Purgatory was just the beginning, you have to stop hiding and face what happened between us."

She jerked her hand from his grasp. "You don't understand, I can't do this. I can't go there again. I might not recover this time."

The tightness in her voice, the fear she trembled with, slid through him, reaching out to every protective instinct in his body.

"You can't deny yourself forever, beautiful, you'll go crazy with it. If not me then someone else. Maybe Dex?"

"No. Dex is safe. I trust him to give me the one little thing every month to get me through until the next time."

"And how is that working out for you?"

Her silence told him all he needed. It wasn't. For someone like her, being submissive wasn't a role she could wear when it suited her, to be shed when her body was physically satisfied. The mental needs were every bit as important as the physical. Something he understood all too well.

"Cass, I don't want to hurt you. I want to push you and demand of you, fulfill you but never hurt you."

Her hands shook as she knotted the rag over and over.

"You have to decide."

Her gaze slid to his, resignation staring up at him. "I just can't. Another freefall would kill me." A sheen of moisture shone from the corner of her eyes.

Frustration speared through him. This denial of hers was going to drive him crazy. Time to put a stop to it. He stood then, grabbing her by the shoulders and hauling her against him. Swallowing her gasp with a brutal kiss. His fingers grabbed at her hair, pulling some of it down and tugging at the loose strands. He breached her lips, pushing his tongue between silken skin to dominate the warm recess of her

Eliza Gayle

mouth. A fist of desire punched at his stomach, taking his breath and hardening his dick. Touching her like this in public was a dangerous risk but she'd pushed him, convincing him this was the last resort. If this would be the last time he saw her he was damn sure going to remember it.

Molding her frame to his, he rubbed his erection across her clit in the subtlest of moves. She'd feel it but no one watching knew for sure what he'd done as long as she remained quiet. When her tongue curled around his, seeking its own satisfaction he knew he had her.

With a strong tug to her hair he tore his lips from hers and drug her head back until her gaze locked with his. The dark hunger there pleaded for more, something she would have to come for if she wanted.

"When you close tonight I want you to come to me, my sweet brat. We both deserve this chance."

She nodded.

"I won't beg you, it's not my way, but I do ask that you give me the opportunity to prove myself as a man of my word. I vow to never leave you hanging. To allow you to suffer in need."

When she began to speak he pressed a finger to her lips. "We're done talking. I'm leaving my card on the table and whether you show up tonight is all the response I require." With that he plucked the paper from his pocket and dropped it onto the smooth surface.

He strode away, confident he'd see her again. At the door he slid a glance to the bar and noticed all three employees frozen in place, mouths agape. Outside in the sunshine he bit back a smile. He'd look forward to hearing how she explained that little scene.

* * * *

Walker stalked to the bar in the corner of his living room and poured two fingers of straight Scotch. He glanced at the clock for the fifth time in the last ten minutes, the pit in his stomach growing into a weighted lump that wouldn't go away.

Cass' shop closed more than two hours ago and so far he'd not heard a word from her. Anger grew inside of him, not at her, but instead at himself for allowing his arrogance to get the best of him. It was hard to deny the way she responded every time he touched her, but parlaying that into something more this fast had clearly been a mistake.

He'd either have to let her go for not showing up or rethink his strategy for getting her to open up. He swallowed the amber liquid, letting the burn going down sooth away the rougher edges of his disappointment. Still the memory of her body pressed against his as she begged for more would not release him. Instead it clawed at his insides like a hungry beast desperate for escape.

Walker slammed the glass onto the bar and headed for the kitchen. He'd skipped dinner while preparing the basement and drinking on an empty stomach didn't seem like a good idea at the moment.

His heavy boots sounded on the wood floors, loud enough he almost missed the soft chiming of the doorbell. Frozen in place, a warm surge of arousal rushed through his veins. She'd decided to come after all.

He beat feet to the front and swung the heavy door wide open. Sure enough, Cass stood on his porch with a nervous smile on her face, turning his night back around.

"I almost didn't come." She spoke softly, her hands clutched together in front of her.

"But you did."

Her slight nod lit something inside of him. The deep, feral side that required his utmost control. He needed to not push her away but she'd come and she knew exactly why.

"You know why you're here?" He stepped forward and cupped her chin, smooth soft skin caressing his fingers. Lifting his hand, he tilted her head back until their gazes met and locked. If he wasn't careful he could get lost in the shimmering need swirling there.

"Yes, Sir."

"Be certain because I won't ask again." He stepped back to give her room to enter if she so chose. His groin tightened from looking down at her in simple jeans and a snug white cotton t-shirt. She'd forgone wearing a bra and tight, beaded nipples strained against the fabric. The first thing he had to do was get her out of those clothes.

Some of the fear clouding her features fell away as she stepped forward and into his home. A soft hip brushed against him, sending a jolt of lust straight to his dick and more wicked thoughts of what he wanted to do to her.

She wandered into the living room with him right behind her. He needed her to be comfortable and didn't feel the need to rush her...yet.

"You've got a great place here. I love the colors."

"Thank you." He favored a natural, earthy style to his house and had decorated everything in browns and greens. He hadn't wanted to hire a decorator, and honestly this had been about as creative as he could get. Now the basement was an entirely different story and he couldn't wait to see her reaction.

"Did you do it yourself or hire a decorator?" He swallowed the smile that would have told her he knew just how nervous she was and that he liked it, but he didn't want to encourage anymore.

She'd stopped in the middle of the room and he stepped close, within inches of her backside.

"You don't have to be afraid," he whispered in her ear.

Her shoulders sagged a fraction before she responded. "I'm nervous."

"I won't hurt you." Never would he do something she didn't want him, too. "In fact you should settle on a safe word now."

"I'm not worried you'll hurt me, at least not

physically."

Walker grabbed her shoulders and whipped her around to face him. Anger and something else flashed through his chest, something not to be unleashed. "I know a little about your past, although not nearly enough. Tell me."

Cass blew out a hard breath. "There isn't as much to tell as you'd think." A muscle in her jaw clenched when she ground her teeth together. "I was with my Master for a couple of years, living as a slave. I went pretty deep. Giving myself to him completely on a twenty-four seven basis."

"There's nothing wrong with that, if it made you happy."

"I know," she agreed. "I was happy. Then one day I came home and he was gone. No explanation, no release, just gone." Cass pulled from his grasp and turned away. "I know what you're thinking. There had to be a sign, something happening to give me a clue and maybe there was. But I didn't see it. I trusted him so deeply I wasn't looking for a signal things weren't great for him."

"Cass...," he warned before grasping her wrist. "Don't put words in my mouth I haven't said. "We aren't supposed to rely solely on signals and body language in a relationship." He rubbed his thumb along the soft skin of her hand. That slight touch started a buzz of need between them. "Communication is key. If a Dom or sub can't talk to each other they shouldn't be together."

"I don't want to repeat the mistakes of the past," she whispered.

"Then don't. That doesn't mean not trying again though. What some ass did to you in the past was completely wrong and will not be repeated here." He sucked in a breath, exhaling slowly before he continued. "One of the worst things a Dom can do is to leave a sub to freefall. It's beyond cruel and unforgiveable in my book."

Wet tears shimmered in her eyes as he leaned forward and kissed them one by one as they escaped. "You're safe here," he murmured. His lips continued to caress her cheeks as he traveled toward her neck. The soft, pliant skin there smelled like peaches and tasted of pure woman. Once again the need to possess her and protect her welled inside him until he wanted to burst with it.

He pulled abruptly away from her and strode in the direction of the bar. "Can I get you something to drink? Beer or wine perhaps?" He needed a few minutes to gather himself so as not to be led by the cock straining for freedom. The urge to pound into her until they both came in ecstasy would never be more important than his submissive's needs. So right now they'd take a few moments.

"I'll take a white wine if you have it."

"I do." He reached into the hidden refrigerator and pulled out his favorite Pinot Grigio and poured her a small glass. He had no intention of allowing her to get intoxicated. He wanted her fully aware and participating in their fun.

He moved around the bar and handed her the glass. "Would you like a tour?"

She nodded and sipped eagerly.

"First..." He grabbed her drink and set it down on the table. "I want to get a look at you."

Her gaze went from curious to shimmering mischief in a matter of seconds as her bottom lip curled into her mouth and between her teeth. Her little girl look made him harder.

"Strip." The innocent face faltered as fear crept back in. After a few long seconds and his unwavering stare her hands moved to the hem of her shirt and bunched it in her fingers. With slow and precise movements she lifted the fabric to reveal her tanned stomach and the underside of her breasts.

His breath caught in his lungs as he struggled to maintain his cool. Her hesitancy and fear riled up the Dom in him and he couldn't wait to see how far he could take her, even tonight.

"Off." His command came out harsh even to his own ears but she got the message loud and clear and pulled the shirt over her head and dropped it to the floor. The ice hard nipples atop her perfect breasts looked like cherries on his favorite treat and he longed to suck them into his mouth. She'd look amazing with a set of clamps screwed onto them.

His dick leapt in his pants at the mere thought. Fingers trembled at the waistband of her jeans as she pulled the button and zipper and slid them down slender legs. His mouth went dry at the sight of her shaved little pussy.

Damn.

She straightened her back keeping her head bowed and her eyes cast downward.

"So beautiful." His fingers reached for her, cupping one breast feeling the weight in his palm. His thumb circled the nipple watching it tighten and pucker. The ruby red tip beckoned and he bent his head to suck it into his mouth.

Her shoulders relaxed a fraction or two as his tongue swirled and licked before gently biting down with his teeth. Her low moan spurred him on as his other hand pinched her free nipple tightly between his fingers. Her gasp at the sudden burst of pain echoed through the room and he smiled against her flesh.

Her hands reached up and threaded into his hair and he pulled away. "Hands down. No touching for you yet." Her eyebrows drew together and a little pout formed at her mouth but she did as told and dropped her arms to her sides.

"That's not fair."

"You're in the wrong place if you expect fair. Good, painful, exciting and likely thrilling for us both, but never fair."

Her frown deepened, giving him cause to laugh. She looked upset but the moisture he'd glimpsed at the top of her thighs told the true story. To prove his point he slid a finger through her soft folds.

"Damn, woman, you're so wet." He spread

the cream and increased the pressure of his rubbing up one side and down the other. Her hips jerked every time he got near her clit and didn't touch it until a series of whimpers tumbled from her mouth. He didn't want her to come just yet. Soon though, very soon he'd watch her come for him over and over again until he'd taken her as high as he possibly could. Only then would she become his and he hers. Dom and sub.

Pulling back, he watched her face. Eyes squeezed shut with such a fierce determined set to her mouth as if she could will him to give her what she needed. She knew it wouldn't happen until he was good and ready but she'd still try. Submissives like her always did. Even experienced ones who'd been away from a dominant man for a while had trouble giving into control, relinquishing that last shred of self that would allow them to quit worrying and just feel.

Her eyes languished open when he stilled his hand a second before moving it away. The look of pure drugged arousal told him she was ready for the next step.

"I think we'll save that tour for another time."

She nodded in agreement as her body swayed towards his. Time for the dungeon.

Walker led her through the kitchen and down the short flight of stairs to the finished basement below. The pride and joy of his home. Besides the elegant colors of chocolate and cream he'd used, he'd outfitted the luxurious space with anything and everything a man like him could need to carry out every submissive's fantasy. From the spanking bench in the corner, to the custom made platform bed with cuffs at every corner as well as dangling from various intervals in the canopy, this room had it all.

"Wow."

A sidelong glance in her direction showed her focused on the St. Andrew's Cross in the corner. Not surprisingly he'd figured she would like that apparatus the most. The setup was similar to Dex's space at Purgatory. In fact, he and Dex had played with a fun little sub here a few months back to try it out.

"You have everything here. You don't even need the club."

"Everything but the right submissive." He winked at her and she blushed the brightest shade of pink he'd seen in a long time. How could something like that throw her off? He still didn't understand why she underestimated her appeal to a Dominant. It's times like these he'd gladly take her old Dom out to a whipping post and beat him silly. No woman should be made to feel inadequate.

"Cass, do you wish to submit to me tonight?"

Her beautiful eyes settled on him. "Yes, Sir," she whispered.

"Do you trust me enough to put yourself in my hands? To give you what you need whether you're sure of that or not?"

She nodded.

"Based on what I saw at Purgatory I know that you don't shy away from pain, that in fact pain is very much part of the pleasure that you need."

He led her toward the big cross but bypassed it at the last second and instead walked her onto the platform built up in the middle of the room.

"Cass, look at me." She raised her gaze to his. "Are you prepared to use your safe word if you need to? To tell me what you need if you aren't getting it?"

A subtle shiver worked through her as he nudged her legs apart in the middle of the platform.

"Yes, Sir. I am ready."

"Excellent. Tonight you are getting restrained, I will have nothing less than all of you once and for all."

She stood stock still as he buckled the cuffs around her ankles and then raised her arms over her head and repeated himself with the leather straps around her wrists. He stood back and studied her when he was done as she pulled on the chains, testing her ability to move.

Satisfied the chains were taut and she had little range of movement he walked to the wall and selected his favorite flogger. The soft leather handle molded to his palm and the thick strands consisted of a variety of braided red and black knotted leather.

"How do you feel?"

"I—uh—nervous."

"Good. Losing your freedom can be disconcerting as well as freeing."

He lifted the flogger and dangled the ends across her shoulders, tickling her bared breasts. The tips hardened to such sharp points he wanted to clamp them. They'd have plenty of time to explore every toy he owned, for now he'd test her tolerance for the wicked ends of his flogger.

Her breathing increased with every stroke against bare skin, her spine ramrod stiff as she waited for his next move. With a gentle flick he wrapped tendrils around her thighs, teasing close to her labia.

Back and forth between her legs he repeated the movement until she sighed with the pleasure of it, letting her head fall backward. She wanted more and he aimed to please her. Making sure she had what she needed was the most important mission of the night. Breaking down the last of her barriers that held her back.

No more freefalling for his little sub. She deserved so much more.

He moved across every inch of her from breasts to arms and legs, to the shapely curve of her ass he couldn't wait to explore. No pain yet, only pleasure. Caress after caress until she strained against her bonds for more.

"More?" He didn't really expect an answer, it wasn't necessary. Although begging never hurt. He smiled at the way she looked at him, lust gripping her.

126

Eliza Gayle

With the sudden twist of his wrist he slapped the leathers against her with more force, enough for the ends to bite into her skin. She jerked forward on a long low moan. Oh yeah, she needed this more than she'd admitted.

He started to hit her in rhythm, a solid figure eight pattern going up and down her body. She cried out when he caught her nipples and thrashed against her chains. Soon her skin turned a nice rosy pink and her harsh breathing changed to pants. A light sheen of sweat covered her and quivers of pleasure jerked through her.

"You've been hiding yourself from me. Too afraid to take a chance. Why?" He walked behind her and struck her ass, his dick jerking at the sight. "I haven't hid my desire for you even a little." One blow after another he continued to work her over, her moans getting louder. "Do you not want another Dom?"

Cass' head shook violently from side to side as he listened to the distinct sounds of a woman on the edge, dying to come.

"No, you don't want a Dom or no, you do?"

"I do, I do," she managed on a ragged moan.

Walker moved forward taking her mouth in a savage kiss. Eating at her with everything boiling inside of him. Blood raged through him as his finger went to her soaked folds, sliding inside her. Harsh and rough he plunged into her, avoiding the swollen clit she so desperately wanted him to touch. Satisfied with how close she rode the line, he withdrew and stepped back to resume the whipping.

This time his wrists moved hard and fast, no doubt increasing the pain she felt. She surged forward, never flinching away, seeking more and more from him. Her dark hair plastered around her face as she thrust her breasts up in the air. God, he loved her responsiveness, her need for his rougher touch. She would be the perfect submissive.

"Do you want to be my submissive, Cass?" He struck against her nipples then, a sharp lick at sensitive skin. Her moan turned to a wail as she arched forward.

"Yes, I want..." She gulped in air, trying to catch her breath.

Finally... He tossed down the flogger and wrapped his arm around her waist. He pressed his lips to her shoulder, gently as she trembled in his arms. "You've given me quite the gift tonight." Her eyes fluttered open. "Your free submission was all I wanted."

He reached to unbuckle her arms first, one by one undoing them and rubbing the chafed skin of her wrists.

"Can you stand?"

"Yes," she whispered.

He knelt at her feet and undid the bindings at her ankles massaging the tender skin and encouraging the muscles in her calves to relax.

He scooped her in his arms and carried her to the bed, shudders wracking her shoulders the whole time.

He quickly shed his clothes and tossed them

to the ground, aching need coursing through him to be with her. Inside her. Stretched out next to her he smoothed his rough hands across her soft body, rubbing at the marks he'd left on her skin. His marks.

"I need you, Cass. Every bit as much as you need me."

A cry caught in her throat, tearing at his heart.

"No more waiting, no more avoiding. I will have you now and you'll know the truth."

He pulled her legs apart and settled over her, his cock pushing at her wet pussy. There was no need for any more preparation, she dripped wet and hot from the whipping.

She reached for him and he grabbed her arms before she could, pinning her to the bed with his hands and his hips.

"No," he growled. "My woman, my way."

He thrust into her then, burying himself to the hilt between the tight squeeze of her muscles and scraping against her clit.

On a high-pitched scream she came for him, her whole body shaking underneath him.

"Fuck!" He couldn't hold out against the sensation of moist skin tightening around him like a clenched fist opening and closing trying to milk his release.

"Damn it, woman, you drive me mad." His hips bucked uncontrollably as he rammed into her over and over again. One scream turned into another and he didn't know where one orgasm stopped and the next began.

"Mine now. Every day. Whenever and wherever I want." Walker plunged again as energy sizzled up his legs and into his balls. One last desperate push and his spine tingled as he emptied into her, hips flailing in abandon.

Walker collapsed over her releasing her arms and taking the brunt of his weight on his forearms. Sweat covered him and tears ran down her face.

Worried, he pulled from her body and tucked her head into his shoulder. "Beautiful, why are you crying, did I hurt you?"

Her head shook against him. "Not sad. Happy."

He smiled and savored the feelings she stirred inside him. He'd found the woman he didn't know he was looking for, the woman who with her lush body and sensitive vulnerabilities had taken a piece of him as her own.

"I hope you know I'm keeping you."

Her head lifted from his shoulder, her dark gaze settling on his. "I wouldn't have it any other way."

Burned

Chapter One

"Hey, Ruby, how's it going?"

She glanced up at Lance, her coworker just long enough to give him a dark look before she threw her purse behind the bar and shoved onto a barstool. Being late drove her nuts and no matter how casual the job it never left a good impression. She'd been hoping for a few minutes of quiet to pull her thoughts together before the club opened.

"That bad, huh?"

"You have no idea." It had been the kind of day that made her want to go back home and crawl under the covers, and instead she was here in Purgatory preparing for a long night of tending bar. First, the fire she'd been assigned to inspect that morning had torn through her like a white-hot poker lance, reminding her far too much of the past. The damage it had caused left a devastated family in its wake and the investigation was panning out to be one hell of a challenge for her to figure out. Her stomach rolled.

"You see the schedule for tonight yet?"

"Yeah, I saw it a few days ago on my last shift." She needed to find some headache medicine.

Lance shook his head and slid a sheet of paper in her direction down the smooth wood top of the bar. "There's been a few changes in the entertainment since then."

"Whatever, I still have a busy night ahead of me and I'm not here for the entertainment." Purgatory was a strange cross between a goth nightclub and a fetish studio where club goers indulged in some elementary BDSM play or spent their night on the dance floor with some intense techno tunes. To keep things hopping there were also stage performances every hour on the hour. "As long as the tips are good I'll be happy." She didn't have time to focus on anything but her job for the next several hours.

"You might want to take a look."

Ruby stilled at the warning tone of his voice and turned to look at her assistant for the night. Her gut twisted at the carefully schooled features of his face. "Why do I have a sudden feeling you're trying to tell me something I'm not going to like?"

Lance shrugged and walked away from the bar. "Let me know when you've cooled off and I'll come back."

Ruby rolled her eyes and plucked the paper from the bar. Lance was so dramatic. After the day she'd had, how bad could it be? She'd been working here for over a year now and this wasn't exactly her first charity event. These nights typically included everything but the kitchen sink and they'd all been well prepared for it. Gabe had explained more than once that by offering so many options he'd draw twice the number of people than a regular night, and so far he'd not disappointed her.

His predictions were always spot on.

She skimmed the schedule, not seeing anything out of the ordinary until she got to the bottom. There, in bold red pencil, someone had scribbled the name *Zane*.

She felt the blood drain from her face and her head spun. She couldn't tear herself from the word and her brain repeated his name over and over. Unbidden images of strong muscles and knowing eyes filled her head. Lips made for pleasuring and a too confident smile every time he looked at her, as if he saw deep inside her to secrets she didn't even know she harbored. Of all the damn people in this town, why him? No, there had to be a mistake. Gabe had told her personally Zane would not be attending tonight's event when she'd agreed to take the head bartending position.

"What kind of bullshit is this?" She spun on the stool and found an empty room. The cowards had dropped a bomb on her and ran. Neither Lance nor Gabe were anywhere in sight.

"I'm leaving, you hear me? You promised and I trusted you," she shouted to the empty room.

"Aren't you being a little melodramatic?" Gabe's voice boomed over the sound system.

"He's just a man, after all, and since you refuse to tell me what happened to cause this hatred, what am I supposed to do? We had two acts cancel at the last minute and his group was the only replacement I could find that was worth a damn."

"He's the most arrogant bastard in this town. God's gift to Domhood, my ass."

"Careful, Ruby, I'm beginning to think getting the two of you together might not be such a bad idea," Gabe mocked.

She clenched her jaw and ground her teeth. The sudden urge to break something flooded through her. Why did the mere mention of his name set her off? Because his cocksure attitude grated on her nerves, but the voice and body got her panties wet every damn time he was near.

She sighed. "It would serve you right if I left now."

"You won't leave me in the lurch. It's not in your nature."

Ruby propped her elbows on the bar and dropped her head into her hands. She didn't know whether to tug her hair in frustration or run from the building. Without warning, her thoughts wandered to the first time she'd met Zane. She'd happened across his fire demonstration at a private after hours club by chance and she'd been immediately drawn to his flame. For as long as she could remember the beauty of the myriad colors and the radiating heat had mesmerized her. But Zane... She'd never met someone so in tune with the fire with every look—every move. With every passing minute she'd found herself moving closer until she'd ended up a few feet in front of the most incredible man she'd laid eyes on. The beat of the music matched the rhythm of the fire and the movements of his body. He'd led her onto the stage and proceeded to use her to explore the different implements of pleasure that could be utilized with fire. By the time he got to the bullwhip her mind had been driven into a frenzy, her panties were soaked and the fact she'd needed him to fuck her had become a foregone conclusion.

Ruby bit down on her lip at the memory as she fought to control the shiver working through her. Her heart raced and her breathing grew labored. As much as she wanted to forget the affect he'd had on her, thoughts of him always did this to her. And was exactly why she did not come to the club any night Zane performed or demonstrated.

She'd have to find a way to avoid him, that's all. As long as he kept his distance she'd be fine. She'd get through the night with her self-respect still intact and her skirt firmly in place.

She could do this. With bills looming she really needed the money a night like this would earn. She stood and turned to face the DJ booth above the stage. "You keep him away from me, you hear? If you don't then I won't be responsible for what happens."

"Sure thing, Ruby, whatever you want. Consider it done." Gabe laughed.

Instead of reassuring, the sound seemed sinister, even foreboding. Nothing like a bad feeling to start off one of the biggest nights of the year. She scooted around the end of the bar and began rummaging through supplies. She needed to have everything in place before the event started. If Gabe's predictions were correct they'd have a record-breaking crowd tonight. Maybe keeping busy would keep her mind off the man she'd hoped to never lay eyes on again.

Her boss had asked her more than once what her issue with Zane was all about, but how could she explain something she didn't understand herself? Every time she heard his voice stroke her skin her insides melted. The hard lines of his face coupled with the aura surrounding him scared the shit out of her. No, the fact she wanted to obey when he spoke frightened her more.

He thought he was a gift to submissives everywhere, and on some level he wasn't wrong. Women flocked to him, eager to be his next conquest. His reputation preceded him, and no one questioned anything he did. Self-confidence was one thing, but what Zane possessed spoke volumes. He vibrated with an innate power that had a profound effect on everyone he came in contact with. To her it flashed like a neon sign warning her to stay the hell away.

She didn't consider herself submissive, nor did domination appeal to her. Most of the activities here in Purgatory did little to excite her...except one. From as far back as she could remember she'd been hyper focused on heat and fire. There was a certain wonder that fascinated her. How could something that caused so much destruction and harm also be one of the most beautiful things she'd ever seen? Her curiosity to learn every aspect of why and how it worked led her to volunteer as a fireman way back when, but her propensity to want to play and explore kind of conflicted with the primary goals of a firefighter. She sat back on her haunches and let more memories take her away.

The blistering heat and flames taller than herself should have sent her scurrying from the building, or at the very least served as a warning that the fire was out of control. Instead she stood her ground and watched it burn, allowing the calming effect to steal over her. She wanted to reach out and touch it, understand it. The danger meant nothing, only the desire to be close and feel its heat penetrating her suit.

When her partner and boyfriend at the time had drug her from the burning building she'd discovered the eroticism of her obsession. He'd fucked her that night while memories of searing heat and bright orange and yellow flames flitted through her mind. She'd fractured into a release that both frightened and entranced her. The boyfriend had dumped her and insisted she needed therapy, and she'd agreed. How could this fascination be normal?

She'd sought a counselor with an open mind who directed her onto a path that turned into a remarkable transformation. First she'd urged Ruby to consider fire investigation instead of trying to fight a fire. Definitely not her forte. With her deep desire to understand how a fire burned, her therapist felt certain she'd enjoy the puzzle of an investigation. Second, the woman had recommended a fetish club where she could meet other fire fetishists and learn to use the attraction in positive and safe sexual ways instead of feeling guilty for an attraction—that while outside the "norm" as defined by some, it wasn't all that unusual.

Now in her second year as a fire investigator, she loved her day job immensely. She had a knack for science as well as an intuition for understanding the aftermath of a fire scene. She'd only taken the gig as a part-time bartender at Purgatory so she could hang out here without feeling like an outsider. While most of the club goers had a strong interest in pursuing the BDSM lifestyle, she'd never had an interest despite her mother's role as a full-time slave to her father. Quite the opposite. The struggle to understand what made her parents happy had taken its toll over many years.

The barren shelf where empty and ready glasses should sit caught Ruby's eye. She'd have to go to the kitchen and retrieve them herself. Whoever had closed last night had done a piss poor job of pre setup. Ruby pushed to her feet and swiveled to face the room, her gaze traveling to her favorite booth. She'd requested to work the second floor bar so she could keep an eye on the fetish stations. For a charity event Doc would pull out all the stops, and on her break she'd hit him up for some fire play of her own.

Despite her lack of interest in BDSM as a whole, they'd welcomed her into the Purgatory family and embraced her fire fetish. Doc had taught her some of the basics and frequently offered to teach her more, but she'd shrugged him off. She understood fire and, while she could probably wield it well, it wasn't where the desire lay. Gabe had tried to explain that she continued to display submissive tendencies but she didn't want to listen to his theories anymore than she wanted to think about her reoccurring dreams.

She wasn't her mother. She desired an equal partnership that gave her the freedom to explore her unusual attraction to fire. Was that really too much to ask? Ruby shrugged and pushed her way into the kitchen where she loaded three trays of freshly washed glasses for her bar.

The door swung open and John sauntered in. "Hey, Ruby, I didn't know you'd be here tonight."

She flashed him a quick smile and stacked the trays on top of each other. "Yep, Gabe asked me to head up the second floor so here I am."

"I'm surprised, I thought with Zane—" He clamped his mouth shut and turned beet red.

"Yes, I've heard that Zane will be here. Jeez, did everyone know but me?" *And does everyone know I have an issue with him?*

"Would you have agreed to work tonight if you did?"

They both knew the answer to that, and she wasn't about to satisfy it with an answer. "As long as he stays away from my bar we'll all be just fine."

"Uh huh...like last time?"

"I admit I might have acted a little out of character then, but that doesn't mean anything. The man just knows how to set me off."

"More like push your buttons if you ask me."

"I didn't, so let's not talk about him anymore."

She hefted the trays into her arms.

"Hey, let me help you with those."

"Nope I've got it. Ex-firefighter, remember. You're in charge."

"Yeah, yeah, you never want any help, I've got it." He pushed and held the door open for her. "Good luck tonight. I have a feeling you're going to need it."

Ruby swept through the door, ignoring John's last comment. What the hell did he know anyway? She started for the stairs and detoured for the elevator at the last minute. No need to push her luck.

A quick glance at her watch showed it was already after eight. She'd have to hurry before the rest of the staff and some of the early birds started trickling in. Now if she could just ditch the nagging feeling in her gut that tonight wasn't going to turn out like she expected all would be right with the world.

* * * *

She was the epitome of everything he desired. Strong and willful, beautiful and mysterious. Zane Michaels watched Ruby as she rushed to the bar and shoved the trays across the counter. Her hand swept a thick lock of hair from her eyes, and her lips puckered and blew air into her bangs. He imagined a trickle of sweat sliding down her flushed cheeks as she swiped across her jaw. His cock leapt in his pants at the sight. If he thought he'd been aroused on his way to the club from the anticipation of seeing her again, it compared little to the raging burn in his body now that she stood across the room from him.

He'd been thrilled to accept the offered gig from Gabe with the one caveat that she had to be there. Their last encounter had been seared into his brain and she'd never been far from his mind since. She'd been entranced by his show and he recognized a fire fetishist when he saw one. Sure, plenty of the submissives allowed the fire play he desired, but none of them craved it deep down to their soul like he did. Nor did they have any desire to be pushed by his limits. He knew how to get them off on command and many of the pain sluts cherished their time with him, but something had always been missing. He'd found it in Ruby's beautiful eyes that night and he'd not been able to forget it. The way they'd widened at his command spoke volumes.

Eliza Gayle

There had only been a spark of hesitation before she'd instinctively obeyed. *Submissive.*

She'd danced with him and his fire, entwined together in heat that should have scared her but didn't. Instead her body had softened under his touch like sweet, soft cotton candy that melted in his mouth. She was a daring and bold woman who'd instinctively trusted his guidance and experience, and the moment his hand slid under her skirt to find sopping wet panties their fate had been sealed forever. At least in his mind. Ruby didn't seem to agree, and for that he'd done his best to honor her choice, but the memory of her exploding in orgasm on his table was forever seared into his thoughts. She appealed to him so much that he couldn't stop thinking about her. He'd bided his time over many weeks and waited until the time felt right to take another chance with the defiant beauty.

Zane focused on her now as she worked to set up for the night. She bent over the bar to reach for something and her tiny skirt rode up the backs of her thighs until he swore he spotted a glimpse of red panties underneath. Her legs were thick with muscle but disappeared quickly into bright red fur covered boots. Even the clothes she wore to the club mimicked the appearance of fire, making him harder than he thought possible.

"Damn," he cursed under his breath. She had no idea the extent of how she affected him. But somehow some way before the night was over she'd understand in crystal clear

Technicolor.

"If she catches you watching her like this she's likely to tear strips off your hide with that sharp tongue of hers." Gabe settled into the seat next to him, yet neither took their eyes off of her. When she adjusted the knot just under her breasts a quiet groan slipped from Gabe.

Fierce protectiveness rushed forward and Zane clenched and unclenched his fists in an effort to stay calm. There'd be a lot more men than Gabe eyeing her tonight, so it wouldn't do either of them any good for him to act like an ass before he got a second chance. He had a feeling one wrong move and he'd be watching Ruby's back as she ran for the door. Unfortunately, the white schoolgirl style shirt she wore tied above the waist and unbuttoned to the swells of her tits made it more than obvious to anyone who looked that she wore no collar, making her fair game to every Dom in the club.

"Did you tell her?"

"Yeah, I made sure she knew when she came to work tonight, but I've kept my distance ever since. She's not happy and I don't understand why. What happened between you two? I believed you when you told me you wouldn't hurt her, but she's so on edge at the news and I feel responsible."

"She's scared." Truth be told he was a little nervous too. Getting past the barrier's she'd erected was critical and he expected would be quite a challenge in one night.

"Yeah, right. Our Ruby is scared of nothing. I've gotten the impression that she's one hell of a daredevil." Gabe leaned against the table behind them. "Got herself let go from the firefighter training program a while back because she took crazy risks."

Interesting. "It's the fire. We both know how much she loves it, but she gets too close and loses control. She needs a Dominant to lead her."

"She says she's not a submissive and has no desire to get involved with a Dom. She's been clear about that since the beginning. Adamant in fact."

"Have you ever asked her why? I think the lady does protest too much..." Again the memories of her reactions pressed down on him.

"Zane, I don't like that look in your eye. What are you up to and what can I do to stop it? She's a great bartender and I like her a lot. I don't want any trouble tonight."

He swiveled and glanced at his friend. "I already told you I wouldn't create a problem. Trust me."

"Uh huh. Famous last words." Gabe lowered his voice. "Now tell me something else that doesn't make me feel like locking her away from you tonight."

Zane stared at the back of Ruby's head, longing filling him to the bursting point. "I need her as much as she needs me. She's the one."

"Shit. You're in love with her. What a

freaking mess."

He didn't bother to answer because it wasn't really a question. Did he love her? He wanted to take care of her, he certainly ached to own her, but he didn't know enough about her for more. Yet...

Gabe stood and faced Zane. "She'll go for the fire tonight. She's too antsy not to."

He nodded. "Exactly what I'm counting on."

Gabe took one long last look at Ruby and shook his head. "I trust you, man, but if you hurt her..."

Zane ground his teeth at his friend's warning, holding back the urge to question him about his interests in her. It was obvious Gabe cared about her, but the odd look in his eyes he kept trying to hide made him wonder if there wasn't more. He and Gabe had enjoyed their fair share of women together but he had no intention of sharing this one. Ruby would be his and his alone. It's what they both needed.

Chapter Two

She peered into the crowd amidst the haze of fake smoke and the neon lights coming from the performance stage seeing nothing but a sea of faces she didn't recognize scattered among some of the regulars. The crowd had surpassed Gabe's expectations, and she'd been running ragged all night long. Every hour a new group had come on stage and she'd held her breath, hoping not to see Zane.

Now the crowd at the bar had thinned to almost nothing, which meant only one thing. The main act was about to start, and she had an unobstructed view of the stage. *Just great.*

She busied herself with gathering the empties and either throwing the bottles in the recycling bin or stacking the glasses on the trays she'd arranged in the corner. With any luck she wouldn't even notice the show. Yet the moment the first streaks of fire lit up the darkened club Ruby turned, unable to stop, and stared. She was doomed.

The girls were first, and she reveled in the

familiar glow and imagined the heat streaking across her arms every time one of them stroked her skin with a firestaff. Chills raced up and down Ruby's spine and her hands shook with rising need.

Who was she kidding? She couldn't not watch. She made a beeline to the other bartender to tell him she was taking a break.

"Yeah, yeah. I know. You want to watch the show." He grinned. "I don't think I'll ever understand your fascination with fire."

Ruby shrugged. He wasn't the first person to say that. "I've always loved it. The heat, the beauty. It's mesmerizing."

"Uh huh. And painful."

"Half the time I don't even feel it that way. I focus on my breathing and the warmth. All it takes is the right person wielding it to make you soar."

"I think I'll take your word for it." He waved her away with his hand and she moved towards the stairs. She didn't have to worry about the crowd—they'd all moved front and center of the stage as she made her way through the staff area to the side. She'd be able to watch unseen from here and would have plenty of time to get away before anyone spotted her.

Another woman had joined in, this one a spinner using two implements lit on the ends. Neither of the women wore more than pasties over her nipples and the skimpiest of panties that hid very little. Not only did it draw the crowd, but it cut down on accidents happening if your clothes caught fire. Annoyed with herself, Ruby shook the thoughts of fire safety from her head and focused on the actual flames.

The heat only ran along arms and legs for a split second, but she moaned every time. It wasn't hard to conjure the memory of the delicious warmth on her own skin as the fire caressed her body. How long had it been since she'd last played? Forget Doc, she'd definitely have to look up Gabe tonight and see if he was up to a nice long session after hours. She'd save the payback for setting her up for another night.

Zane walked onto the stage and yanked Ruby from her thoughts. His presence invaded her from head to toe. Her nipples tightened painfully and her sex squeezed sharply. She hadn't exactly forgotten how breathtaking he was, but time had allowed her some distance. No longer.

Firelight gleamed across his shaven head and lit up the multitude of tattoos that emphasized his bare torso. Muscles bunched and flexed in rhythm with the music so she almost missed the glint across his pecs. *Oh, wow, that was new.* He'd added nipple rings since the last time she'd seen him. As if he needed anything else to make him hotter. She forcibly closed her gaping mouth. If she wasn't careful she'd be drooling long before his show ended.

Not that she'd come to see the man.

He carried his personal fire staff and moved closer to the women, maneuvering the flames over and around their writhing bodies in an erotic dance. The fire from all the implements swirled and swayed until they blended and the eye could no longer tell where each one started or where they ended.

Before long her body thrummed and pulsed in sync with their movements as she stood mesmerized. When the girls switched out their tools for the short fire breathing sticks, Ruby turned her focus to Zane and his performance. His movements seemed effortless, but she knew better. He kept his gaze on the fire at all times so he could study its patterns. He controlled it, dominated it every second.

As much as she didn't want to admit it, she'd never seen a fire performer with his natural abilities. He probably understood fire even better than she did. Yet he'd taken the time to learn to wield it as if he'd been born to it. Gabe had a proficiency for fire play like nobody's business, but his skill paled in comparison to the possessive style Zane exhibited. What would it be like to let him control both the fire and her pleasure? If only he didn't want to force her submission...

Her chest constricted painfully. His parting words from their last encounter were never far from her mind.

"Submitting to the fire is the only thing that will make you truly happy. Unfortunately it can't be the fire dominating you, doll. You need a Dominant with enough control to handle both of you."

Distracted by her thoughts, she almost missed the two ladies getting on their hands and knees, heads to the floor and asses high in the air facing Zane. He'd switched from a staff to the fire whip. A tingling sensation raced through her body as he unfurled the flaming tail. A collective gasp rushed from the crowd, mirrored by Ruby. She found herself attracted to the seductive sway of his body almost as much as the promise of heat searing the barred backsides of the women.

Longing rose in her, sharp and swift. Liquid heat pooled between her thighs. She'd never experienced the fire whip since so few people willingly wielded it, but it had centered prominently in her dreams for quite some time. It took a lot of practice to become proficient when the dang thing wasn't on fire. When Zane pulled out the whip, she was helpless to resist.

He lifted his arm and circled the whip around his head, the fire reflecting in the taut flesh of his bicep. Ruby held her breath waiting for the crack she knew was coming. The pop vibrated through the room and a ball of flame bounced from the end of the whip. The murmur of the crowd fed her excitement to the breaking point until Zane landed the first strike on one of the women's backside. Ruby's body grew taut, her pulse pounded in her groin and her breath came in fast pants.

She glanced around quickly to ensure no one

saw her, then slid her hand underneath her skirt. The whipping continued, each stroke fast and furious but enough to leave small red streaks behind. The more she watched, the more everything ached. The slightest movement brushed sensitive nipples across rough fabric and her hand rubbing her panties wasn't enough.

She roughly pulled the silk strip out of her way and plunged two fingers inside her sex. *Not enough. Not enough.* Her head lolled from side to side but her gaze never left the flaming tail of the whip. She wanted to anticipate the next strike but couldn't focus. Her fingers pressed forward, deeper...she couldn't deny the storm brewing inside her.

Ruby's vision narrowed, the scene in front of her eyes taking sole focus. The torches all around the stage, eager moans for more from the two women, and Zane's presence dominated her mind. She didn't always understand how fire and desire went together, but she'd learned through experience never to deny it. To live in the moment.

She allowed her own moans to slide from her lips when she quickened the pace of her hand. The fiery scene existed inside her, aching to get out. Blasts of heat pressed against her skin like a lover's caress, sending blistering need sweeping through her senses. Oh God, she was going to orgasm standing less than thirty feet from the one man she wanted more than breath.

Eliza Gayle

He looked at her then, his gaze boring into hers.

Oh shit, no. Her hand stilled but it was too late.

Come.

Shock rippled through her as he mouthed the word, tearing a scream from her throat. Fast and powerful, her release rippled through her, over her. Her hand fell free and she grabbed at the railing to stop from falling. She gasped for air as the crowd beyond her broke into thunderous applause. This couldn't be happening. What had she been thinking, coming near him?

Her body throbbed and pulsed as she tried to gather her wits. The need she'd created was far from sated, but staying here wasn't an option. Fear seized her. She'd go to Gabe and ask for his help. Yes, he'd help her and then she could go home with her sanity still in place. Gabe she trusted. Zane only led to a path she couldn't afford to take.

Ruby forced herself to stand and straighten her skirt. After a few slow, deep breaths, she gathered her wits and headed back to the bar. She still had a little time left on her shift and she'd have to wait on Gabe to finish his work too. Her hands and arms shook as she raced to the stairs. The crowd would be breaking up and she didn't want to get swept along.

Halfway up the stairs her legs quaked to the point she had to stop and grab the rail to keep her balance. Nausea rolled through her as images of Zane and his fire whip crowded her thoughts. Ruby shook her head and trudged to the bar. Only a couple of customers stood nearby and the assistant bartender stood wiping down the bar.

She stopped and stared. For the life of her she couldn't remember his name. What the hell? Her heart thudded in her chest and sweat broke out on her forehead. Ruby spun around, searching for the source of her distress.

"Ruby, what's wrong? You're so pale."

She couldn't focus on the voice with the sound of blood roaring in her ears. She moved behind the bar and grabbed the low shelf to steady herself. Tears welled in her eyes, threatening to fall. She didn't know what was happening to her. She understood the high she normally got from fire play, but this was far more intense and she'd not even come close to the flames.

"Ruby, seriously, you're freaking me out."

She needed to pull herself together and get back to work, but her heart beat too fast and her head felt like someone had stuffed cotton in it. She was spinning out of control.

"I'm calling Gabe to let him know you're sick."

No. She thought to protest but couldn't form the words. She was helpless to do anything until she recovered. Her clit throbbed as strongly as her pulse, her skin tingled and everything ached for...she didn't even know anymore. Relief, it's all she could think of.

She was fucked.

"Yes, Sir, I will," the bartender responded to whatever order Gabe must have given him. She'd tuned out the conversation so she had no idea what he'd told him, but if she knew Gabe, and she thought she did, he'd be up here in no time.

"Here." Her assistant pushed a glass of orange juice into her hands. "Gabe said you need to drink this before he gets here. I doubt it will be long."

She glanced down at the small glass and shook her head. There wasn't much chance she could hold it without spilling it all over herself.

"Here, I'll set it right here in front of you so you can sip on it when you can. We've got some customers I have to take care of, but I'm right here if you need anything."

He left the juice and moved away. Ruby focused her gaze on the orange liquid and took some deep, slow breaths. How had she gotten herself in so far over her head? She could push through this and everything would be fine. She picked up the glass with a trembling hand and brought it to her parched lips. Cool, sweet juice trickled down her throat, relieving some of the anxiety.

She detested being weak. She was better than this, and the thought that somehow Zane had reduced her to this only proved she had no business being around him.

"Hey, babe, you doing okay?"

Gabe's hand gently touched her back and

smoothed underneath her hair. Relief flooded through her at the simple caress as she tipped her head back into his hands.

"I saw you go toward the stage. What happened?" his breath brushed her ear.

Emotion swelled and broke loose as everything she'd tried to hold in came flooding out. A single tear slid down her cheek and her shoulders slumped forward on a shudder.

Gabe grabbed her shoulders and turned her into his chest, his arms folding around her. The warmth and comfort of her friend surrounded her. Jesus, what a baby she'd become. Somehow she managed to hold back more tears, but Gabe must have sensed a serious problem.

"You and I are going to one of the private rooms until you feel better."

It had not been a question, and she didn't bother to respond. For once she needed to let him do what he thought best. At least until she had herself under control. The heat of embarrassment still flooded her cheeks when he scooped her into his arms and carried her to the private elevator that would take them to the third floor. She caught snatches of random conversation as Gabe ushered the crowd out of his way. God, she'd never live this down.

* * * *

"What the hell?" Zane glared at Gabe's back as he carried his woman off across the club. And yeah, whether either of them knew it she was definitely Zane's, and he'd come to convince her tonight. Not fifteen minutes before, she'd come at his command and then disappeared before he could get off the stage. He wanted to paddle her ass for her behavior.

No way had what happened left her in the right frame of mind. She was as afraid of the truth as she was about letting anyone get too close. She hung close to Gabe because he was safe for her. He'd respect any boundary she provided whether she needed pushing or not. Gabe was a great guy but he'd never be the Dom for his Ruby.

He moved quickly backstage, trying to get to the third floor before they did. A hard smile formed across his face. If she was in need he had to be the one to take care of her, not Gabe. No offense to his friend, but he wasn't what she needed. He took the stairs two at a time and hurried toward the private playrooms. His attention to health and fitness was not only required for his work, but came in handy at times like this as well.

Ruby... The look on her face when he'd spotted her had nearly stopped him cold. Pure, dark pleasure was evident in the hooded eyes, the tip of her head and the tongue that kept licking at her lips. He knew where he wanted those lips. His cock hardened impossibly tight. Damn, he couldn't remember the last time a woman cranked him this high.

He liked nothing more than watching her reaction to his fire, but wanted to take things

Burned

much farther than in the past. He needed to play with her, kiss her, even claim her. Watching her bloom under his guidance and safety would be incredible. The pleasure he ached to shower on her overwhelmed him. He'd waited long enough.

Zane rounded the corner in time to see Gabe unlocking the first playroom. He ducked inside and Zane sped up, his hand slapping against the door as Gabe tried to close it behind him.

"What the—?"

"I want Ruby." Zane shoved the door open and pushed his way inside.

"She's in no condition to handle you, Zane, so back off."

The worry in Gabe's tone startled him. "Why? What's wrong with her?"

"I don't know, you tell me. She went to watch your show and then fifteen minutes later I get a call from her assistant saying she's sick and unable to talk."

Zane rushed to take her from Gabe. Ignoring his friends' protests, he lifted her in his arms and walked to the door, nodding at Gabe to follow. He'd take care of this his way, damn it. Not in some damned cold playroom.

She stirred restlessly in his arms. "Shhh. Just relax and give me this. Please, Ruby, I'll take care of you. I promise." She felt so small in his arms and he didn't miss the slight trembling of her arms and legs. "You shouldn't have run. I could have helped you if you'd given me the chance."

158

"Run? What the hell happened, Zane?" Gabe interrupted.

"Not here and not yet. We can talk in the car. For now let me take care of Ruby."

He admired the soft lines of her face while he examined her for signs of trauma. The color in her cheeks looked good and the fluttering of her lashes had slowed. Even some of the tension he'd first felt in her rigid posture had given way to his touch. Achingly beautiful. It was the only way he could think to describe her. Long, sable hair that grazed her ass when she stood, small breasts with nipples that stayed hard all the damn time, and full hips that cradled him perfectly.

He took the backstairs so he wouldn't have to walk her through the crowd. It was nobody's fucking business what he was up to and he didn't need to deal with any other protectors. Besides, his car was right outside the door. He dug into the pocket of his leathers, pulled the keys to his car, and tossed them to his friend.

"You drive."

"Zane, I can't leave, I've got to close up soon." He stopped and blocked Zane at the door.

"Jesus, Gabe, I don't live five minutes away. You can't spare that much time for her? I'd drive but I'm not letting her go at the moment. It's that important."

Gabe glared at him skeptically, but he must have seen the desperation Zane couldn't hide. The woman in his arms drove him crazy. A combination of strength and tenderness grabbed him by the throat and didn't let go. There had to be a compromise that would work for them both, but not until she recovered and he taught her a lesson or two about taking care of herself.

Gabe unlocked the vehicle with the remote and Zane opened the rear door to his SUV, slid onto the seat, and closed the door behind him.

He held her tight. The night air had chilled and neither of them had a lot of clothing on. She sighed contentedly and he relaxed into the cool leather seat. "You remember the way, don't you?" Sarcasm clung to every word, but Gabe had tried to thwart him one time too many so his annoyance ran high.

"Yeah, I remember..."

With Gabe glaring at him in the rear view mirror, he returned his attentions solely on the woman in his arms. He sank into the soft, warm skin of her arms and legs. Needing to maintain close contact and wanting so much more.

He'd yet to fuck her, but they'd come damn close the last time they were together. Had it not been for Gabe interrupting, she would have been naked with him buried so deep she'd never get away from him. Something his friend had eventually regretted. A rough sigh escaped his lips and she in turn squirmed in his lap. She'd settled enough she had to know what she rubbed against. *Sweet fucking agony.*

"Be still, Ruby. You're not ready for that and I'm only human."

160

Eliza Gayle

He had to bite back a smile when she instantly froze. He moved his hand from her ass and lightly massaged her leg until once again she relaxed against him and her breathing returned to a soft and steady cadence. This fear of hers had to go.

He stared at Gabe, who sat stiff as he drove the car, and caught his gaze when he glanced quickly in the mirror. "Our girl here sure likes the fire, doesn't she? It took her over in an instant."

Gabe sighed and nodded his head.

"How long's it been since the last time?"

"You know this isn't about sex for her," Gabe whispered.

"Don't insult me. I know exactly what she needs and I also know she's been living on the fringe, just getting enough to maintain her secrets. She isn't satisfied." He raised his hand when Gabe started to speak. "I'm not trying to insult you. I'm sure you've done as much as she would let you. Which is the crux of the problem, isn't it?"

"She's adamant about not being submissive to me. It makes a difference on how a session can go."

Zane snorted. "Is that what she keeps telling you? And you believe her?"

"Look, man, I know you've got a massive hard-on for her, but at Purgatory we have rules and we don't cross them—ever."

"Which is why I'm taking her home."

"I don't know if that's such a great idea. I

161

don't think she's ready for a Dom like you. Probably never will be." Gabe raised his shoulders and titled his head to the side.

Tension filled the car and Zane wanted to ignore it. But if he didn't deal with it then Gabe would never leave her alone with him.

"You know it's a little freaky to be sitting here listening to the two of you argue about me as if I'm not even here."

Her voice startled him. She'd begun to recover a lot quicker than he expected. That she did so in his arms was a damn good sign.

"Just looking out for your safety is all," Gabe answered.

She pushed to a sitting position and opened her eyes. "If that were true then maybe you wouldn't have asked me to work tonight. You set me up and now you're feeling guilty about it."

Gabe started to deny it and stopped. Ruby was no pushover, that was for sure. She pushed against Zane's chest. "Let me up."

"No."

Her brow arched. "Excuse me. Did you just say no?"

"Yes." Fiery anger lit her eyes and color infused her cheeks. He waited for the backlash that would soon follow. That she had gotten riled up over the conversation was a clear indication she was getting back to normal.

"I cannot—"

"Don't you even understand what happened to you?" Zane interrupted. "You need to rehydrate and take it easy for a while."

"I'm not a child, and I hardly think a bout of low blood sugar is cause for all this." She waved her hand around the car and he bit back another smile. Jesus, he loved her spirit, her determination. And especially her strength. The one trait above all others attracted him to her.

"No, you're definitely not a child, and I'd like to suggest again you stop squirming in my lap." His cock twitched against her bottom and she looked at him with sheer horror plastered across her face.

"What? I've got a beautiful woman sitting in my lap who, as I recall, masturbated in front of me and who knows who else just a short while ago."

"Ohhh—" She fought powerfully against his hold and pushed herself from his lap to the seat next to him with just her wrist manacled by his hand. "You son of a bitch. Let me go."

"I already said no. I'm going to make sure you're okay and then we're going to see about getting you satisfied. Then we can discuss the terms of our future."

Wild fear filled her gaze as she twisted her head to Gabe and back again. "What? Have you lost your mind? I need to get back to work and then when everything is all cleaned up I'm going home. Alone."

"You're not going back to work tonight. Everything's already being taken care of," Gabe broke in. "Zane's right. You may think you're fine, but twenty minutes ago you scared the hell out of several people."

Ruby sighed, some of the anger clearly deflating. "I'm not sure what happened and I'm sorry if it freaked you out, but really, I think I'm fine now."

Zane tugged on her wrist and pulled her a little closer. "I'm not leaving you alone tonight, so you decide. We can either go back and spend the night in a public playroom, or you can come home with me. My preference would be a warm bed at my place where you'll be comfortable and private, but it's your choice."

Silence stretched out between them as he imagined her thinking through the pros and cons of his offer. He'd known she wouldn't like her options.

"I don't like being manhandled." She leaned forward to the front seat. "And as for you, I don't even know what to say. How about we take door number three and you can take me to my place."

He pulled her back against the leather. "No. Not an option. You didn't have a blood sugar issue back at the club, so clearly you either have no idea what you're doing when you get involved with fire play or you're in some major denial."

Suddenly her elbow connected with his gut and his breath whooshed from his lungs. She'd caught him off guard just enough to again slide away from him as close to the window as she could get. He'd tensed, readying himself for a fight when she turned her head to gaze out into the night, not saying a word. They rode like that for a few minutes until Gabe pulled up to his building and killed the engine. For a few long minutes no one spoke as the tension in the car rose. He was prepared for her to yell and fight him.

Yet once glance in his direction and Ruby didn't look mad anymore, she looked...sad.

"I know a lot about this kind of thing...first hand. I grew up with it."

"You discovered your fire fetish when you were young?"

"Yeah, but that's not what I'm talking about. I didn't understand the attraction to heat, and it took years before the craving for it started to twist me up inside." She ran her hand along the edge of the window, her movements slow and distant as if she were lost in thoughts or memories.

"Let's go inside and you can get comfortable. Then we can talk about what happened."

She looked at him then—a blank look in her eyes. "I can't be what you want," she whispered. "I don't know how many ways I can say it before you finally understand."

He banked down the surge of anger at her words. This was no time to push. There would be time for that later. "Don't judge me when you haven't even talked to me. Our only encounters have been in clubs where we both are in a different zone." He opened the door and held his hand out to her. "How about we not jump to conclusions about each other tonight and just see where this goes?"

He counted the seconds in his head as she watched him carefully. It was clear how unsure she was but it had to be her choice and he wouldn't force her to comply. His stomach jumped when her hand reached for his and he closed his fingers around her and helped her from the car.

"Hey, Gabe, thanks for bringing us. I'll send someone for the car tomorrow."

"No problem—but, Zane, if you hurt—"

"Don't do it, man. Don't be a cliché here. You know me and you know she's safe." After a few seconds, Gabe nodded his head and Zane slammed the door shut.

"How are you going to get your car back?"

"No worries, beautiful. It's taken care of." He steered her toward the building entrance and she looked skyward.

"You know, I've wondered what the inside of this building looked like. I did the investigation on the original building after it burned down. It was damned good to hear they were going to rebuild it and keep many of the original specifications. It's always sad when the city loses a landmark to tragedy."

He let her chatter nervously on about his building, only half-listening. His focus remained on her, and how the change in topic affected her. Her color brightened and her eyes were alive again. The passion that she had for her job, tantalized him at the same time it eased a good bit of tension from her demeanor. Good, maybe now she would be able to relax with him, because this wouldn't be an easy night for either of them. He had a few lessons to teach and one way or another he'd find a way through her defenses until she agreed to give him a chance.

Chapter Three

Ruby wolfed down the last of the cookies Zane had given her. The man had no idea of the sweet tooth she possessed, nor the fact that his having her favorite peanut butter cookies in his cabinets had raised him a few levels in her eyes. As if the man needed to go any higher. She hated admitting that there was probably more to him than she'd allowed herself to believe.

He paced the apartment, restlessly waiting for her to finish. Now that her sanity had returned she no longer wanted to talk about what happened. But they were alone, and she was quite certain a man like Zane wasn't going to let things go. Yes, he struck her as being prepared for anything at any time. So far, he kind of reminded her of a leather clad Boy Scout with a surly attitude.

Unfortunately her train of thought led her away from her hunger for food, and had given way to an entirely different hunger. Ruby swallowed the last of the cookie and shook her head. She needed to get laid. It was not hard to admit that she'd wanted him from the first time she'd laid eyes on him, but this need now clawing at her insides was ridiculous.

Sure, the fire had been her first attraction, but the man behind it was every bit as magnetic. Tall and muscular, with broad shoulders covered by a black T-shirt that clung to a heavily muscled chest and rock hard abs. If that weren't enough to make her rub her legs together she remembered well the light trail that disappeared into his pants that rode low on narrow hips. The man wore leather like she didn't know what, but it made her want to touch him, no...rub all over him. Just watching him perform, observing the way he moved, had taken her obsession to a higher level than ever before.

The pants were snug and cupped his cock just right as if saying come and get it. And, judging from the bulge she'd found herself sitting on in the car and the other times she'd pressed against him, she would not be disappointed. What was it about him that made her want to throw caution to the wind and give in to all her wicked thoughts? Where exactly has her resistance fled to?

"What?" he said, his voice rough.

He'd turned and caught her staring. She liked the gruff expression on his face—a cross between complete frustration and desire. Their chitchat had done little to dissuade his erection and she couldn't be more excited. She slid from the stool in his kitchen and moved slowly toward him. He must have sensed she was up to something because he took a couple of steps backward. She stalked closer.

"I'm feeling much better now." *Although she was hungrier than ever.*

"You look better." He touched her hair, then the side of her neck.

"I've tried to deny whatever this is between us for a long time now. I'm tired of fighting." She lifted her hands and unbuttoned her top. One after the other she slid the tiny buttons from their holes and untied the knot from beneath her breasts.

"We need to talk about what happened earlier."

"Actually, for the first time I think we can wait on the talk." She removed her blouse and dropped it to the ground.

A distinct groan sounded from Zane. "You are a little minx who needs to learn a lesson or two. Your denial is going to get you into serious trouble."

"Maybe...maybe not." She reached for the button of her skirt and unfastened it. Her fingers grasped the zipper and ticked it down nice and slow. She spied his hands clenching and unclenching in fists and the muscle at his jaw tic. Her plan was having an effect.

"You're definitely a dangerous woman who needs to learn control." He took one step in her direction.

"I think I'm doing just what needs to be done. After all, we've been avoiding this for a while now." Her hands grasped the fabric and skimmed it down her hips and thighs until it pooled at her feet. The ache between her legs grew tenfold when his eyes widened in appreciation.

She raised her hand to touch him.

"Don't. Move."

The command was barely a whisper, but swept over her with the force of a fully involved fire. Her body froze and awakened. Her nipples puckered to tight points and moisture gathered at the opening of her sex.

"Mmm. So submissive," he drawled.

Ruby's heart immediately kicked into overdrive. She tried to back away, shaking her head. "Don't say that."

"It isn't a dirty word you know. In fact, there's so much strength in your submission it humbles me."

Ruby averted her eyes and grasped for the right words to make him understand. She wanted him so bad right now. But how far could she let this go before it blew up in her face? Backing out now would kill her.

"Just this one time?" she asked.

The scowl on his face deepened for a split second before it smoothed out and the corners of his mouth lifted ever so slightly. "You think one night will be enough to get me out of your system?"

Ruby barely refrained from rolling her eyes. Hotness aside, the man had an arrogant streak a mile wide. "You talk too much. The more you analyze the more I want to leave."

"Sassy mouth." He pressed two fingers to her lips. "You need to be sure about this, because once we start, I won't be stopping."

Zane's fingers skimmed across her jaw, along the outside of her arms and finally on her stomach. His rough, scarred hands left a heated trail of pleasure everywhere they touched. Every bone in her body melted.

"I like watching you perform. It turns me on."

"You like me, or the fire?"

"Both," she admitted. "But right now there is no fire..."

"Damn, woman, you're making me crazy. One minute I want to turn you over my knee and the next I want to be buried inside you. You're not logical."

She leaned forward until her jaw brushed his neck and her lips grazed the curve of his ear. "Then take me. Please."

Something broke between them and he grabbed her around the waist and lifted her. Automatically she wrapped her legs around his waist and dug her fingers into his arms. God, his muscles, his warm skin, and the smell. The scent of burning fire covered him, filtering through her senses. She moaned helplessly in his arms as he carried her to his bedroom.

Together they fell to the bed, him landing on top of her with his erection pressing against her heated sex. He was so hard. And big. Satisfaction warmed something inside her that felt suspiciously outside of simple lust. His hips shoved forward, halting her wayward thoughts as he dragged his length across her clit. Pleasure sizzled through her, her nipples tightening to aching points and moisture coating her labia.

"Oh, Zane. Clothes, please. I need to feel skin. Need to feel you."

He chuckled and bit the soft skin in the curve of her neck. The sudden pain zinged inside her, bouncing from one pleasure zone to the next. Her nerve endings fired and a long moan erupted from deep inside her.

He lifted enough to shove her thong to the side and grazed his fingers across her lower lips. Whimpers tore from her throat as he fed first one long finger inside her and then a second.

"Fucking hell. You're so hot." He pushed his fingers high and her eyes rolled back in her head. She couldn't think, couldn't breathe.

"Yes," she cried out.

Without removing his fingers, Zane lifted from her and grasped her hip with one hand and pulled her forward. "Jesus, Ruby, you're so beautiful." His face lowered until his heavy pants pushed his breath across her dampened flesh.

She arced her hips and he smiled.

"I'm going to take my time, baby. You're going to come so many times you won't be able to think straight." Warm heat pressed against her clit and Ruby screamed. His tongue pushed and prodded until his teeth took over nibbling on her most sensitive flesh.

"Ohhh, ohhh." Fast and furious, her orgasm rushed over her. An explosion of pleasure grabbed a hold of her and flung her to the stars. Every continued flick and lick with his tongue pushed her farther than she thought possible.

Her hands wrapped around his smooth head and pressed him closer. In response he worked his fingers rougher inside her. Fast and slow, brushing the sides of her channel until she hovered again on a ledge, unable to move.

"I like watching you come. That moment of complete loss of control, when simply feeling takes over the brain and you can no longer fight. It's a place you need to be as often as possible. Then maybe you wouldn't think so hard about what you may or may not be."

It was hard to follow his words with his fingers fucking her, teasing and tempting her. He'd abandoned her clit for the area above his fingers.

"Jesus, you taste good. You've drenched my fingers and still it's not enough. Give me more, Ruby. Come for me again." He curved his movements until he touched just the right spot. Without warning or build up, she convulsed and came, her inner muscles clenching around him.

"Fuck yes, baby. More sweet wetness for me to enjoy."

His hot tongue delved alongside her fingers where he could catch every drop. Her head lolled to the side. How much more of this could she take? She'd thought taking the role as aggressor might change their natural dynamic, but lying here helpless as he ate at her pussy was too good.

"Stop thinking," he commanded just before his fingers touched her G-spot.

She whimpered, her legs spreading farther. His free hand spread her lips wide as he licked a path to her clit. Slow. Agonizing. Zane fastened his mouth over her swollen bud for just a second and her upper body jackknifed off the bed. At this point, her body was so sensitized they were riding the line between pain and pleasure, leaving her torn between asking him to stop and begging him for more.

She needed him inside her now.

Ruby's legs trembled with weakness as he continued to love her with mouth and fingers. He alternated long deep strokes with short digging ones while he blew hot air across her aching flesh. Despite the cool temperature of the room, the familiar sensation of sweat trickled between her breasts. She thought of trying to pull herself together, but she loved the heat inside her too much. She spent so much time wound tight, afraid of her own inhibitions. If she could let go with Zane, maybe she'd find the whatever she'd been looking for. And if tomorrow it was gone, she'd learn to live with it.

"Relax, Ruby, don't stiffen up now. I can tell you're still trying to analyze this. Your job right now is to do nothing but feel. Can you do that for me, baby? Trust me to give you the pleasure you crave."

She looked down at him, at those sharp eyes that never missed a thing, and nodded her head. A slight quirk of the lips turned his serious look into something playful as she felt the distinct sensation of another finger sliding inside. Good God, how many was he using?

She moaned harder as he stretched her with slow, calculated movements.

"Judging by how tight you are, I'm probably quite a bit larger than you're used to, but sopping wet like this you should have no trouble at all."

Her eyes grew big at the thought of him splitting her in two with his cock. Yes, she wanted him, and the longer he delayed the more frantic she got. "Need you inside..."

His fingers eased from her channel and he tore at the button of his leathers. This was it...she was giving in to Zane. The one man she swore she had to resist. Although if she'd ever quit lying to herself she'd have known this day was inevitable. She glanced at his chest and shoulders, the muscles moving fluidly as he removed his pants. Naked, he took her breath away. Where he looked like an escaped chiseled god of perfection, she felt ordinary. Yet the hungry stare he turned on her flipped her stomach. He wanted this as much as she did.

He'd been right about being larger than she was used to. His erection was huge, bigger than she'd imagined. Long and heavily veined with a flared crown already damp with pre-cum. Her mouth watered, ached to taste him. She forced herself to take a breath and dragged her gaze to his face. Her face flushed with heat at the satisfaction she recognized in his eyes. On a small moan her sex squeezed and more juices gathered at the top of her thighs.

In her peripheral vision she saw his arms moving and the tell tale sound of a condom wrapper ripping, but tearing her gaze away from his was out of the question. Even without his fire he mesmerized her. If she'd been standing her knees would have buckled from the crushing desire he inspired. *Mine.*

"Damn, Ruby, don't look at me like that."

"Like what?"

"Like you need me." He pressed a kiss to her belly and butterflies erupted. Did she need him? She wasn't supposed to, but she feared that that it might be too late for that.

She twisted and turned and arched her back as he traveled up her body until the tip of his cock settled between her thighs. "Please, Zane. Don't tease me."

His hips rocked forward, pushing his dick a couple of inches inside her. "Oh, Ruby, you have no idea what teasing is if you think that's what I'm doing now." He surged forward, sinking inside her the rest of the way. The move stole her breath on a sudden gasp. He stilled long enough for her body to stretch and accommodate him before he withdrew partway.

Ruby grabbed his shoulders and wrapped her legs around his waist to keep him seated.

Burned

"Not yet." She gasped again.

"So impatient," he murmured.

"I'm no—" Her protest died on her lips when he stilled above her and swooped in for a kiss.

Warm and soft lips pressed to her mouth, sending tingles into her limbs. "I knew you'd be tight, but damn, woman. How long's it been since you've been with a man?"

The heat of a blush crept up her neck at the memory of her last lover. She wasn't about to embarrass herself with the truth. "A while," she admitted. *A very long while.*

"Do you need more time?"

"No. Please, now." Her heels dug into his ass and pressed him forward, impaling her once again.

"You really don't have much control, do you?"

"Who the hell needs control now?" she argued.

"Oh, babe, you have so much to learn. Good thing we have plenty of time for that." He pulled from her until only the tip of his cock remained to tempt her. "Right now we need to fuck." He tunneled forward, his shaft rubbing against every nerve ending she possessed. Pleasure sparked inside her, hurtling her toward yet another mind-blowing release.

"Oh, Zane. Oh yes."

"Come, baby. Let me feel those muscles clamp around me. Come, Ruby, now!"

The urgent rumble of his voice built the crescendo higher until sparks exploded and her body spasmed in orgasm. Without thought she screamed in ecstasy as he slammed into her over and over again.

"Fuck yeah," he rumbled.

Ruby couldn't think. With her orgasm she'd relinquished control and rational thought was no longer possible. Her breath clogged in her throat when she tried to speak as another wave of sensation built inside her womb. Never had she experienced so many orgasms in one night.

"You are incredible, Ruby. When you masturbated next to the stage I'd never seen a more beautiful sight. I don't think you understand how much control it took not to yell in triumph when you came for me. It's a gift I won't soon forget."

He pumped harder. Sweat built between them, her hair plastered around her face. "You're making me crazy, Zane. Please. More." Her hips jerked to him on every thrust. She stared into his eyes, getting lost in the dark swirl of need residing there. Her nails bit into the flesh of his arms as ropes of muscles flexed underneath her hands.

Intense hunger burned between them as he drove his hips harder. Higher. Pleasure stormed inside her, swirling and building on every stroke. Screams of release ripped from her mouth, tightening her muscles around him.

Zane shouted above her, his cock pulsing with his own orgasm. She clawed at his shoulders, frantic with pleasure. Everything magnified. The weight of him above her. The last thrusts pushing even deeper inside her. Emotion rose, threatened. She'd wanted this for so long despite everything she'd done to avoid it. They shuddered together, moaning in unison on the final thrust.

When he sagged against her, Ruby leaned forward and buried her face in his shoulder. She couldn't let him see the impact he had on her. It was sex. Simple, sensational, sex. Something she shouldn't have to keep reminding herself of.

Chapter Four

Zane held Ruby close, burying his face in the warmth of her shoulder. He'd given her what she asked for and it hadn't been nearly enough. Sex with her, even vanilla sex, was more explosive than what he'd expected. Now, with the aftershocks causing her muscles to tighten around his cock, he wanted her again...and again.

"Do you know how long I've been wanting to do that?" he teased, his voice low and rough.

She nipped at his shoulder with her teeth. "Probably about as long as I have."

Reluctantly he withdrew from her body, her tight sheath dragging across his over sensitized cock. If she'd driven him mad tonight, what would she do to him if there were no barriers between them? He padded across the room to the bathroom and quickly disposed of the condom. He wanted to keep her in his arms, away from anything that could hurt her. The need to possess her swept through him. No, not simply sex. He wanted more from her. Her surrender, for starters.

He collapsed beside her and pulled her into his arms. The craving he'd denied for months still burned inside him. She'd tried to deny him by hiding, but eventually she'd come to him. It was a gift he would never forget. Still, she harbored fear of him inside her and he aimed to get it out in the open so they could deal with it and move on.

"Tell me, Ruby," he demanded hoarsely.

"Hmm?" she mumbled sleepily. "Tell you what?"

"Tell me more of what you started in the car. What is it that makes you fear submission?"

She stiffened against him and he touched her arm in response, tracing the curves in a light, soothing pattern. He never wanted to stop touching her. "You're safe with me, Ruby— always. But you need to help me understand what it is that holds you back." He softened his voice. "You can trust me."

"My mother is a slave."

Wow, that he'd not seen coming. More often than not a submissive would admit to a bad experience at the hands of a novice Dom and on a more rare occasion, an issue with an abusive man. This was new. It did explain a lot though.

Zane propped his head on his hand so he could look at her face as she spoke, his fingers still trailing up and down her arm. He'd tread carefully for now and hear what she had to say. "And?"

"*And*, growing up in a Master/slave

household gives me a unique perspective into the inner workings of the relationship. I know my parents love each other very much, but there were times when their relationship scared the hell out of me. I worried all the time about my mother being lost in my father. Her devotion never wavered no matter what he asked of her or did to her in the name of being her Master."

"What do you mean?" He modulated his voice, keeping the tone low and soft...encouraging.

"Her life revolves around nothing other than serving my father. If she does something outside his established boundaries she begs for punishment." Her eyes closed, as if lost in a memory while she spoke. "She does nothing for herself, only for him. It's all about him. Sometimes it breaks my heart."

"How can you be so sure? One of the basic tenants in that deep of a relationship is a slave's need to please her master. It is how she derives her pleasure."

"I know, Zane, I've heard it from my mother many, many times. She is happy. Serving her master is all her heart desires. Yet..."

"You still don't understand it. You constantly wonder how she could possibly be happy like that." He was definitely beginning to understand her wariness. He knew plenty of people who lived like that, but she was the first person he'd met who'd actually been born into it. Lived with it from a daughter's perspective. She clearly hadn't inherited the heart of a slave

Burned

and for that she struggled with understanding.

"I believe her when she explains how happy she is, but I'm not sure I'll ever understand it one hundred percent. I'm not like that. I don't want to be submissive to a man, I like having control over my life."

"Haven't you learned yet that submission, and dominance for that matter, takes any number of forms? The number of levels and ways to practice is as varied as the number of people you meet on a daily basis. In this case, it sounds like your parents live one of the deepest forms of the life, or what some might refer to as an extreme case. However, one size doesn't fit all when it comes to this lifestyle, and I would think you'd have learned that by now."

Ruby pulled away and rolled onto her back. The puzzled look on her face told him she was considering his words so he continued to touch her, focusing on the rounded flesh of her hip, giving her time to process what he'd said.

"I can't be like her."

"No one said you should."

"But you're a Dom in need of a submissive." She choked back a cry. "I can't be your submissive."

"Yet every time I touch you, you nuzzle closer. You try to hold back but eventually the need to give in wins out. Why would you want to resist that? It's beautiful."

Ruby sighed, a frown forming across her face.

He ran his fingers along her compressed lips.

184

"Don't do that. As cute as you are when you're frustrated, you don't have to fight me." Zane tilted his head and took possession of her mouth. It was going to take more than words to get his point across. His tongue swept inside her mouth, melding them together until he stole the breath from her lungs. He wasn't letting her go that easy. He couldn't. He kissed his way down her throat and licked at the sheen of sweat between her breasts while his fingers rolled and tugged at the nipples until she shuddered in response. Against her hip his cock began to swell again as arousal fired between them.

"There's a big difference between what I need and what your parents share. I'm not looking for a slave. Yes, I'm possessive and controlling, but that doesn't mean I want to control a woman's every move. That's a lot of work and responsibility, and not many Doms truly want to go that deep on a twenty four seven basis."

His teeth bit slowly down on her nipple until she gasped and arched. Streaks of heat whipped through him, lighting him up for more.

"What are you saying, Zane?"

"I'm saying open your mind to the varying degrees of submissiveness and I think you'll find the place you need to fit."

"But—"

Zane covered her mouth. "You don't listen very well." He framed her face and stared into her eyes. Stubborn, that's what she was. And irresistible. "Maybe a more accurate demonstration is in order."

He pushed off the bed and held out his hand. She hesitated for a brief moment, but it spoke volumes. "Ruby, do you trust me that I won't hurt you?"

Without hesitation she replied, "Of course I do, otherwise we wouldn't be here." She placed her hand in his and allowed him to draw her from the bed.

"Then trust me to understand how you feel and still stay open to new possibilities. You've jumped to a lot of conclusions that I think you'll find aren't as accurate as you think."

She tilted her head. "Why are you being so patient? There are plenty of willing submissives in this city who would happily knock me out of the way to get to you."

She waited for an answer, and he realized that no one had tried this hard with her before. He squeezed her hand. "Because when the right woman comes along a man will do everything in his power to prove he's the one."

He led her to the end of the hall to a closed door and reached atop the ledge to retrieve the key. While he lived alone, one could never be too cautious when it came to expensive toys and privacy. The door unlocked, he pushed inside and pulled her with him.

"My playroom."

It wasn't a fancy room by any means, nor was it a cold and unfriendly room. It was large and well ventilated, which were the important things when it came to his brand of play.

There was a cushioned table that dominated the room, and while it did come with straps and cuffs at the ends, he rarely used them. The carpeting had been ripped out and the concrete underneath painted black and sealed. Safety first.

"What do you think?"

She glanced around the space. "There's not much here, although I do like the collection of implements on that wall." She pointed to where he kept everything hung or neatly placed.

"This room is only used for my interests in fire, and is not meant for anything else. Does that surprise you?"

She nodded.

He pulled her hand and led her to the table. "Face down, sweetheart. I have much to show you."

Her eyes searched his face and he held his tongue. She wanted him to push, but not this time. He'd let her set the pace and he'd honor as much of her comfort zone as he could. Nothing was more important tonight than her achieving an understanding that she was more than woman enough for him.

When she climbed on the table he bit back a smile of satisfaction. She couldn't be sure what he'd planned for her, but she wanted it. Whether she realized it or not, she wore a good number of her emotions on her face.

"Good girl."

He picked up a lighter and a candle, placed them on the small stand next to the table, and then went to adjust the lighting.

"I think tonight should be about learning for both of us. I love watching you react to the fire and now I want to delve a little deeper into what's behind it. Are you okay with that?"

"Yes, Zane. It's fine." Her voice trembled.

The buzz of energy between them sizzled and popped from the sound of her voice. The stiffness of her shoulders spoke volumes about her nerves. They couldn't start their session like this. Zane touched her shoulders and cringed at the subtle flinch of muscle underneath his hand. For a second the warmth he'd experienced from Ruby earlier disappeared. The years melted away and he stood in the midst of a crowded BDSM club with a huge chip on his shoulder and an urgent need to touch the fire. To relax them both he began to massage Ruby's neck and shoulders.

"The first time I played with fire, I hurt someone very badly."

Ruby turned her head and met his gaze. The shock he recognized didn't surprised him. He'd not exactly been forthcoming about his life. There was more to tell so he pushed her shoulders back to the table and started over again.

"I was very young and still new to the scene. I wasn't sure what I was looking for but I liked the open minded reception I received at my first munch so I went to another meeting and then one thing led to another and I'd become a regular attendee at the local BDSM dungeon."

Her muscles loosened as he continued.

"The first time I saw a fire demonstration I was hooked. Unfortunately I still thought I knew it all and took it upon myself to have a full fledged scene after minimal instruction."

He hated thinking about what an idiot he'd been but Ruby needed to hear his story as much as he'd needed to hear hers.

"I thought I was smart by negotiating the scene with another young submissive who claimed experience in fire play. The arrangements were made, I purchased and made my own equipment and away we went."

"You trusted her to be truthful," Ruby whispered.

"Yes," he agreed. "And despite contrary beliefs, Doms do not read minds."

She giggled, her body shaking slightly under his continued ministrations. The sweet sound caused a shift inside him. He needed to finish the story.

"What I didn't know about this particular sub was that she needed pain and lots of it. I'm sure I don't have to tell you that pain and fire are not a good mix."

"Mmhmm," she murmured.

Zane focused on the satiny texture of Ruby's skin as he kneaded her muscles one section at a time. "I let her push for more and more not watching as closely as I should for the signs of trouble."

Ruby's breath caught.

"Relax, it's probably not what you're

thinking. I didn't light the poor girl on fire or anything. At least not on the outside. Halfway through the session she turned into a screaming, writhing mess in the throes of a painful memory from her childhood."

Ruby turned into his embrace and stared up at him.

"You hit a trigger?"

He nodded.

"First time out and I ended up traumatizing her."

"But she should have disclosed something like that. Subs have responsibility too."

"I know that now and I knew somewhat then but that didn't stop me from withdrawing for a while."

"A while?"

"You aren't the only one drawn to fire. I thought about it all the time. It haunted me."

Ruby nodded her head as if she understood the compulsion exactly.

"That's how I became a performer. I set out to learn everything I could about fire chemistry and safety and from there I learned how to spend my time with it wisely. One thing led to another and now I've managed to make a career out of it."

He leaned down and brushed his lips across her cheeks.

"The fire I mean. So maybe you and I are more alike than you think."

He let his story linger between them so she could take a moment to absorb what he'd said.

She didn't strike him as the kind of woman who would run from him when he admitted to less than perfect experience.

"Still trust me to continue?" He studied her eyes for fear and almost heaved a sigh of relief when he saw none.

Her hand touched his arm. Zane swallowed and looked down at her long fingers wrapped around his tanned skin.

"I've always trusted you with my safety. It's my own flaws that hold me back."

Ruby was so beautiful and honest. Her dark eyes were full of compassion with a tinge of sadness around the edges. The look made him want to hold her close. He couldn't imagine how he'd feel if he'd grown up watching his own mother serve his father as a slave. No doubt it would cause some hang-ups. He hid most of what he'd become from his conservative family. Not because they would criticize him for it but because he knew how much his mother would worry. And she already worried too much.

Just like Ruby.

Zane cupped her jaw and leaned down to take her mouth. Her soft sigh drifted into him, and her grip on his arm loosened. He savored her soft lips, his mind immediately imagining them wrapped around his cock. Damn. This wasn't the direction he'd intended to head. Not yet. With more disappointment than he'd expected, he released her and stepped back.

He stroked a finger along her cheek. "Are you ready to get started?"

New color flooded Ruby's face before she answered, "Yes, Zane."

"Good. Back in position, hair tucked underneath you."

Zane watched her flip to her stomach, brush her hair out of the way, and finally settle on the cushioned surface. He'd never met anyone he'd wanted so badly as her. It wasn't easy to maintain his self-control in the face of her vulnerability. He moved to the head of the table, looking down at her nude form, his gaze drawn to the swell of her ass. He loved her round, lush bottom. Sure, he had a fire fetish, but if anyone paid close enough attention they might call his fetish something else.

His erection began to swell as he leaned over to grab a handful.

"I really enjoy having my hands on you."

There were so many things he wanted to do to her. Like spread her cheeks wide and shove his dick in the tiny hole. His finger grazed the sensitive spot and he felt her shudder underneath him. She was working so hard to stay still for him. Fuck, he wanted to take her again.

"It's not uncommon for a woman to enjoy submission with the right man at the right time, and still keep total control in other aspects of her life."

Her breath sighed out.

Zane smiled and grabbed a fistful of her hair, pulling her head to the side to bare her neck to him.

"Allowing me to take control in here can be as natural as any other human instinct. If you give it a chance."

He wrapped his free hand around her neck and pressed very lightly against her windpipe.

"Zane," she whispered.

"Be still."

Her mouth closed and her eyes darkened with intense arousal.

"Our power exchange means that you trust me enough to allow me access to your body at my will. Fire or not, I'll call the shots. Within limits of course."

Seconds ticked by until finally, she slowly relaxed.

Satisfied for the moment, he forced himself to let go and turn back to the plan he'd intended. He placed the candle in his palm and lit it, watching the wick flicker and light the room with a soft glow.

"Look at me, Ruby. Look at my fire and tell me what you feel."

Her gaze lifted to the candle and her eyes focused and flared wide. Ruby's lips parted for air and her breath made the flame sway before growing steady once again.

"The color. I always notice the color first because it's so beautiful, not quite yellow but definitely not orange and always the blue to frame the edge."

Her description brought the fire to life, breathing air into the room.

"I like the potential danger of it. The

knowledge that not everyone can master the fire. It's mine to wield, to shape and mold for your pleasure or pain at my will."

He gave her a few minutes to stare at the fire, to build the desire just a little more. When her eyes dilated and he recognized that faraway look she always got, he removed the candle from her sight and placed it on the table.

"Tonight I want to try something a little different. I need you to hear what I'm saying as well as feel the fire. So, in order to do that I need to take away one of your senses."

"I don't—"

"Shh." He placed a finger across her lips. "Flip onto your back for me. Trust me to take care of you, Ruby. I want nothing more than your attention and your pleasure. Do you think you can give that to me?"

She nodded and did as he asked. The exquisite site of her flushed breasts and naked pussy distracted Zane for a minute and hardened his cock more. At this rate, by the time the scene was over he suspected he'd be in some pretty serious pain.

"Now lie back and close your eyes. I'm sure you'd want to obey me and keep your eyes closed, but let's make this easier."

He grabbed a black cloth from the bin under the table.

"I'm going to blindfold you." He placed the cloth over her eyes. "You have nothing to fear. You are perfectly safe," he murmured while tying a knot at the back of her head.

He wanted to take this nice and slow despite the urgent arousal growing in his belly. What he needed to get across was far more important than just two people getting off in a scene. Although, he had every intention of making sure his Ruby left in the morning the most satisfied woman he'd ever seen.

He paced to the cabinet behind him and grabbed the supplies he would need and arranged them next to her. He spied a slight tremble in her arms.

"Are you cold?"

"No," she uttered.

"Don't be nervous. I'm going to talk you through every step. Right now I'm getting everything I need together. Nothing to worry about."

He poured some alcohol into the dish and grabbed the smallest fire stick. He dipped it thoroughly; making sure the cotton fibers soaked a good amount of the liquid.

"I love the way you look at the fire, babe. The joy on your face is immeasurable. It's a rare thing, but I understand it well. It's a trait I've waited a long time for. Someone who could understand the intensity I feel about the flame, the color, the heat. You have it in spades."

He dipped the tip of his stick into the flame and sighed at the fast flare of heat and light he created.

"I've waited for the right submissive who understood it wasn't really about the pain. No, fire play is meant to be sensual with a slight edge of pain that enhances the love of the rest."

"But I'm not really submissive," she protested.

"Aren't you? How do you feel when you see the fire? No, not the arousal or the excitement, tell me, when it's just you and the fire, the need coursing uncontrollably through your body. Who's in control? You or the fire?"

He tapped one of her pointed nipples with the flaming end of the fire stick before she could answer. Her back arched and she gasped, her mouth opening and her tongue peeking out.

"No, Ruby. Don't tell me what you think I want to hear, or your off the cuff answer. Think about it before you tell me because I want the truth, damn it."

She shook her head a few times before she finally spoke. "The fire."

"That's right. Isn't that why you're a fire inspector instead of a fire fighter?"

"I love the puzzle of a fire. I need to figure out the why of it."

He touched the flame to the other nipple, making sure to wipe it away quickly.

"That's not an answer. Yes or no, Ruby. Nothing else."

"Yes."

"Good girl. You and fire love each other, that's evident to anyone who watches. But it's your loss of control that we're talking about. Your inability to know when to say when."

"I know enough not to hurt myself."

"You think so? You think if I touched this

flame to your aching pussy, you could make yourself get away when you needed to?"

"No, of course not. I'm not the administrator, you are."

"So if I was lying on this table and our roles were reversed, could you control it?"

"Yes. I know how to handle fire."

"Again, not what I asked. Let's try this another way." He swabbed her belly in an S pattern with the alcohol and touched the fire to it, igniting a streak from belly to breast. His free hand quickly followed, extinguishing it. Her hips rose and she writhed in the pleasure of it. The heat had left the first of many red streaks to come. They were just getting started.

"When you're standing here entranced by the fire, watching it burn, are you going to have enough control to not go too far?"

She hesitated. "I think so. I would never hurt you."

"No, I don't believe you would. Not on purpose, anyways. But fire is magnetic and you, babe, are drawn to it uncontrollably. I see it in your eyes every time, not to mention the way you move. What I'm trying to say is that what works for you and what will bring you the greatest pleasure each and every time is for you to submit. Submit to the fire. And in order to do so, you have to submit to the one wielding it."

He dipped the swab stick into the pot again and drew a line down the side of her hip. Close enough to her pussy for her to feel the heat all the way to her clit, yet far enough away she wouldn't be able to come.

Flame lit up the streak in an instant and he put it out almost as quick, but the effect was done. A loud moan fell from her mouth and her hand reached for her pussy, which he pushed away.

"Mine," he growled. "Only I will be doing the touching tonight. Your only job is to listen and feel. Got it?"

She nodded, her breath coming in soft pants.

"Spread your legs."

That she complied immediately burned through his gut, making his cock ache for more. How could she not see the surrender she gave so freely? The moist flesh between her thighs beckoned to him. Zane clamped down on his inclination to move on. Fuck, he wanted nothing more than to shove his cock inside her. The need clawed at him like a wild beast until his head spun. Not yet. She needed a little more time and way more heat.

"So beautiful, Ruby. Do you have any idea what seeing you like this does to me?

He stroked her leg, loosening the tight muscles she'd clenched in anticipation of his next move. "I don't even have to touch your pussy to know how wet you are, I can see it."

"Yes, Zane," she breathed.

He lowered the swab across her untouched leg and followed quickly with the lighted stick. The area burst into flame, burning the alcohol vapors that hovered above her leg. Most people had the mistaken misperception that the flame actually came in contact with the skin, but it wasn't. Only the heat of the burning alcohol did unless, of course, someone was stupid enough to leave it there too long. He wiped out the flame as Ruby writhed and arched around the table.

"Zane. Please. More. I ache."

"I know you do, babe, but you can go higher."

He rubbed his warm finger over her clit until she gasped, and the fresh scent of her arousal filled his head. She was ready to go off like a firecracker.

"You will listen to me, Ruby, and wait until you are commanded."

He leaned forward to press the crown of his cock against her slick folds.

"Otherwise you'll wait longer."

He hoped she didn't push him to prove that, he wanted inside her too bad.

He tossed the extra swabber onto the tray and moved from between her legs. He tapped the fire stick onto random patches of skin as he walked all the way around the table. Belly, arms, tits and nipples, until he focused the circle around her wanting pussy. He pressed his finger above the hood that did little to hide her swollen bud.

"You want my fire right here, don't you?"

"Oh, God, yes. Zane, please."

"That's why you keep it clean shaven, isn't it? So you can take the added heat where you need it the most."

She nodded frantically.

"Whose fire is this?"

"Your fire."

"And how bad do you want it right now?"

He lowered the flame inches above her flesh until he knew the heat built painfully.

"So bad, please, Zane, you're killing me."

"Good, then you're almost ready."

"Almost?" She choked on the word.

He withdrew the fire and extinguished it. He needed one more thing from her. He pulled the drawer open at the end of the table and withdrew the leg restraints. He'd not planned to use them, but it was yet one more step towards her total submission. To her understanding that he knew best what she needed right now, not her.

"I know your legs have to be uncomfortable dangling like that. Lift your feet and pull them towards you until they are close to your ass." He grabbed one and demonstrated. She visibly stiffened and gasped when he wrapped the cuff around both her legs and locked them in place.

"Zane, what—?"

Her head thrashed and her body shook, she had so little control of herself, even her words.

"Making sure your legs don't cramp. Be still and relax, no one is here to hurt you." He bent and blew a puff of air across her swollen folds.

"Oh, God, Zane, I can't—"

"Yes, you can." He lifted the other leg for her and strapped that one as well. In this position it would be easier to penetrate her deeply without her needing to do a thing. Which was a damn good thing, because the final heated blow would send her rocketing.

He grabbed the implement and dipped it into the lit candle. Fire flamed, the sound rippling around them. Her head perked up and he knew she'd heard it. He popped it on one nipple, then the other. Fuck, he couldn't wait another second to be inside her.

His fingers toyed with the red-hot flesh between her thighs until he couldn't resist another second. He'd teased and tormented them both enough for one night. He removed his fingers and nudged the opening with the crown of his cock. Moisture coated him, easing his entry into the snug passage. Her breath caught in her throat as he forged inside, the clenching muscles gripping him and his control until he slammed the last few inches forward.

Her back arched as her muscles tightened like a vise around him, sending a wave of pleasure shuddering through him.

Fuck, she was so hot.

"You're mine, damn it. You need this. Hell, I need this. I need you and your submission. Submit to me...now."

If the look in her eyes wasn't enough, her physical reaction to his words told him everything. One more clench like that and he'd be done. Sweat beaded on his brow as he struggled to hold still, holding the fire above her clit once again.

He leaned forward and yanked the cloth from her eyes. "Look at me. See who's in control.

Submit, Ruby."

Her eyes stared down at him. "I submit, Zane, I submit."

Filled with satisfaction, he touched the flame to her pulsing clit for a split second. Her scream of ecstasy was the sweetest fucking sound as she tipped into orgasm. He tossed the stick into the safety pan and grabbed her hips. Muscles clenched and tightened around his dick as he began to shaft her. Her tight grip on him made it impossible to achieve long strokes so he angled his hips upward and continued with short, forceful digs. Cum boiled in his balls as his release gained momentum. Ruby screamed each time she squeezed around him until he couldn't hold back any longer.

"Oh hell, Ruby, too much. Too good."

Agonizing pulses of pleasure ripped through him as his release broke free. Hips bucked wildly on each jerk of his cock.

"Cum harder, Ruby." His thumb attacked her clit and she screamed his name. The sheer force of her muscles clenched on his dick milked him dry, leaving them both a shuddering heap.

Long moments later, when his fried brain began to function again, he lifted his head and stared into the gaze of his new submissive. He was so proud of her strength. Now if he could only find his.

"Jesus, woman. You trying to kill me?"

A small smile teased her lips as he moved to kiss her belly.

"I didn't know."

"I know you didn't, but I did. You may not need to be a full-time submissive, but in here, yeah, you need this as much as I do."

"So what does it mean?" Her fingers brushed across his neck.

"It means that I'm going to fuck you six ways to Sunday every chance I get, and then you're going to beg me to do it again."

"And the fire?"

He pressed his lips to the soft, rounded flesh of a breast. "Oh, trust me, when it comes to you and me, we all three go together...It's meant to be."

Chapter Five

When Ruby woke the next morning, her body protested movement. Every muscle, every joint and hell, probably every hair follicle ached from the night before. She rolled toward Zane to find an empty spot. A strange sense of loss cut through her straight to the quick. Their night was over and now she'd have to face a new day with a radically different perspective.

A quick check of the bedside clock confirmed she had just enough time to get back to her place for a shower and fresh clothes before she headed to work. She had a new investigation pending that she hoped to keep her busy and her mind off of Zane.

Yeah, right.

She cleaned up and headed into the kitchen. Maybe she could find some more of those awesome peanut butter cookies he'd plied her with last night. As soon as she walked in the kitchen she spied a plate of said cookies and a glass of orange juice waiting for her. And a note.

She picked up the note first.

Had to leave early for a meeting with a potential client. Thought you might like my idea of a breakfast for champions before you head off to work today so I left these for you. I'll be busy most of the day but how about dinner tonight? I'll cook. Meet me here at six o'clock.

Oh, and Ruby, thank you.

Z

A smile wider than a lake crossed her face, making her wince. God, even that hurt. She laughed out loud as the memory of Zane's cock buried to her throat reminded her why her cheeks were sore this morning. He'd pushed her, no, pushed them both through most of the night until she'd literally passed out on him. He'd proven his voracious appetite for fire play and sex matched her own.

But what now? He'd asked her to dinner but she didn't want to assume that meant anything serious. Her stomach clenched at the thought of not seeing Zane again. She simply wasn't equipped to make this kind of decision on only a few hours of sleep. She glanced at the clock and grabbed the cookies from the plate. She needed to leave now or risk being late. She shoved Zane's note in her pocket and headed for the front door. There was just enough time to catch the bus that would deliver her to her front door.

The rest of the day Ruby combed through the debris and devastation of the McCormick house looking for clues that would lead her to the source of the fire. Fortunately the family had gotten out safely before the fire consumed their lovely home. Still...the loss of everything you owned in the blink of an eye knocked a person flat and left children scared to close their eyes at night. The family in this case only made her push harder to solve the case. If they were left hanging for long, the insurance company would drag their feet and more chaos would ensue. She had people to protect.

Her mind also often wandered to Zane and the delicious memories of the many ways he'd tortured her body. A wisp of heat warmed her insides. Many times through the night he'd called her his submissive and for the first time in her life she began having second thoughts about the true meaning of the word for her.

A glint of fading sunlight winked in Ruby's vision. She glanced at her watch and realized she was late for her date.

Shit.

She jumped to her feet, losing her balance and crashed to the ground in a pile of soot and debris. *Dammit!*

Ruby stood and tried to brush her clothes clean. Instead the soot and ash burrowed into her clothes and covered her hands. Jesus, what a mess. If she went home first to get cleaned up she'd be over two hours late. More reason to hurry. She rushed from the building and jumped in her car. Half way to her apartment she changed her mind and drove to Zane's place.

A few minutes later, she stood mussed and anxious in front of Zane's door waiting for him to answer. Excess energy zinged through her body as the anxiety and worries from her day crashed in on her.

Zane opened the door with a scowl on his face. "You're la—."

"I'm sorry. I lost track of time in the investigation, and when I noticed that the sun was going down I lost my balance and I fell and now I'm a crazy mess and I wanted to go home and clean up, but I didn't want to leave you hanging any longer. Really, I'm so sorry. I thought about dinner all day long and have been looking forward to talking to you." She heaved a sigh.

A wide spread across his face. "Are you done?"

Before she could answer, he put his arm around her and pulled her close.

"No. I'm fil—"

"Stop talking, Ruby."

In an instant, his command caused some of the stress she'd been suffering drift away. She sagged against him.

"I have the perfect solution. Come with me."

For once in her life she didn't argue. She let Zane lead her into his bedroom where her attention was drawn to the bed they'd occupied together less than twelve hours before. She choked back a whimper as they walked past it and into the master bathroom.

"I think you're going to like this."

He sat her on the edge of the giant tub dominating the room, turned on the water and then went to a panel in the wall. He pressed a button and fire erupted in the middle of the wall separating the bathroom from the bedroom.

"Whoa. I didn't even realize that was a fireplace."

"Uh huh. Somehow I knew you would appreciate that," Zane said as he quickly removed her disgusting clothes.

"C'mon, climb on in." Zane stripped and stepped in behind her. He maneuvered her around until her back rested to his front.

"Why are you being so nice to me? I showed up late and probably tracked dirt all through your condo. Is this all part of the submission game you want me to play?"

An arm tightened around her waist. "No, Ruby it's not a game. Is it so surprising that it pleases me to care for you?" He pressed his lips to her nape. "This is just life."

"What does that mean? I thought we were just having dinner but this feels like more than that. But how can so much change in just twenty-four hours? That's crazy, right?"

"I've been waiting a while for you so it's been agonizingly slow for me. You were right when you said I wanted a submissive."

"I knew this was too good to be true. I'm going to go now." She tugged, but his embrace didn't give. Tears sprang to her eyes. Sitting naked in the tub with the man she craved left her too bare—vulnerable.

"You didn't let me finish. I want a submissive who will submit to me sexually like you did last night."

Last night had been incredible for her. "Not all the time?"

"I'll probably be a tad overprotective at times. It's the nature of the beast."

Ruby smirked. "In case you haven't noticed. I can hold my own when I need to."

"Bring it on, babe. I relish the challenge."

No I don't want this. She could see herself falling in love with him and then where would she be? Way too risky.

"You're incorrigible. And just looking for a reason to do something crazy like spank me."

For a moment his lips brushed over her ear. "You say that like it's a bad thing."

"It is."

The words came out of her mouth but there was no heat to them, all the blood had rushed to much lower parts. His hand had begun a trail to her pussy and the more he talked to her the hotter she got.

He stroked her clit and played with her ear until her legs shook with an impending release.

"You don't play fair," she whimpered.

"Nope not fair," he replied before he shoved two thick fingers inside her. "But always fun."

"Oh God!" she cried out then bit her lip in a lame attempt to regain some control.

"Tell me you don't want me," he taunted.

She shook her head wildly from side to side.

"No, I don't want you." Her head dropped back against him.

"Liar." His thumb vigorously rubbed across her clit and Ruby lost her mind. The scream started at the same time as the explosion.

"Mmm. Now that's the way to end a hard day."

"Yes, your tub is really nice." She was damned grateful he couldn't see the huge grin on her face.

"Such a smart mouth on a pretty girl. I think I'll have to give you something later to keep it occupied."

Ruby blushed. He could turn her on in ten seconds flat. No, make that two. He made her laugh when she least expected it, and he'd even convinced her to hate her least favorite word a little less in one night.

They finished their time in the bath in companionable silence. She imagined he had as much thinking to do as she did. After he'd thoroughly washed her she turned and faced him and returned the favor.

"You aren't at all what I expected you to be," she blurted.

"Do I even want to know what you expected?" He wrapped his arms around her once again and pulled her down on top of him.

Ruby shook her head. "Probably best that you don't." She'd been so wrong. He wasn't just a self-centered egotistical ass looking to keep a woman under his thumb at all times like she'd originally pegged him for.

She wiggled her bottom until his cock head slid through her lower lips and prodded her opening.

"Ruby..."

"You can't have control all of the time," she replied.

She eased down his solid length, reveling in the way he stretched her. Fully seated, she clamped her thighs around his legs and started up a rigorous rhythm. She watched his eyes widen but it was the rough groan that melted her insides. He was gorgeous and he wanted her.

His hands gripped her hips but he made no move to take control, letting her set the pace. It didn't take long for the heated need to build to a near frenzy. Her body tightened and her clit throbbed as her orgasm raced forward. She was sooo close.

Zane tightened his hands and forced her to still. She shook so hard from need she wanted to cry.

"You're so beautiful. Stay with me."

Desperate for him to let her move again she'd say just about anything he wanted. "You're being mean Zane."

"Aww, poor baby. The mean Dom wants her to wait," he mocked. If he didn't have a gorgeous grin on his face she'd have been tempted to knock him sideways.

"Please, Zane," she begged.

Her grinned and lifted her body until only the tip of his cock remained inside her. With a protest hovering on her tongue he slammed her down, driving into her with enough force to send tremors shooting through her. And then he did it again and over and over until her body went on overload with no more coherent thought than the delicious fucking he was treating her to.

Ruby clawed at his chest and writhed uncontrollably in his grasp. The hunger inside her grew hotter than any fire she'd experienced. Suddenly the mass of pressure exploded and waves of pleasure crashed over her, sending her into an unrelenting bucking frenzy that made her head spin. Soon thereafter, his groans joined hers when he took his release in a series of hard, forceful thrusts.

Ruby melted into a boneless pile on Zane's chest and savored the rough breaths they shared as their heart beats slowly returned to normal. The aftershocks continued for several minutes, making Zane jerk every time her muscles clamped down on him. The way he reacted to her made Ruby feel powerful. He'd asked for her submission and driven her to new heights of pleasure that sent her out of this world. But lying here now, with his hand stroking her back she didn't feel helpless at all. She rather enjoyed the varied ways he went out of his way to make her feel special.

With a smile on her face she lifted her head. "What's next, sexy?"

Zane lifted her until their gazes met. "There's always dinner."

Ruby frowned and he laughed.

"You worry too much. We are definitely going to have to do something about that." He lifted her off of him and carried her from the tub. He wrapped a fluffy robe around her and tied the belt at her waist. "First food, then we can discuss how we plan to get to know each other better."

Ruby pushed her fingers through her hair and tried to calm her racing heart. She was trembling, and she didn't know why.

"You'll stay with me."

"What?" He'd said it again. *Stay with me.*

He cupped her chin and tilted her head so she was forced to either look at him or close her eyes.

"You didn't really think after gaining your submission last night, I'd simply watch you walk away did you?"

She didn't know what to think. It was all happening so fast. The possessive words. The incredible sex. And the playroom of fire.

He caught her around the neck and drew her close before walking her backward to the wall. She didn't fight or argue because... The truth hit her harder than she'd expected. She wanted to surrender to Zane. Before she could voice her thoughts he had her pinned to the wall and his thigh shoved between her legs. "I think it's time for another lesson in submission. Have you ever been spanked?"

Ruby swallowed. "Can I please have dinner first?"

His eyes sparkled. "Yes, you may. Then you can meet me in the playroom."

Ruby's eyes widened as she thought of the purpose of his special room.

Fire.

He was right. She would never get enough of him and that thought lit her from the inside out. "Yes, Sir. It would be my pleasure." Would it ever.

About the Author

Eliza Gayle lives a life full of sexy shapeshifters, blood boiling vamps and a dark desire for bondage...until she steps away from her computer and has to tend to her family.

She graduated Magna Cum Laude (which her husband translated into something very naughty) from college with a dual degree in Human Resource Management and Sociology. That education, a love of the metaphysical and a dirty mind comes in handy when she sits down to create new characters and worlds. The trick is getting her to sit still.

...Join her in her world. The door is always open and the next red-hot adventure is just a page away.

Look for Eliza on the Web at http://www.elizagayle.net or check out her blog at http://www.elizagayle.net/blog.
She is also on Facebook at http://www.facebook.com/AuthorElizaGayle and Twitter at http://www.twitter.com/elizagaylebooks

Continue reading for delicious sneak peeks!

Afterword

Thank you so much for reading *Fetish Dreams*. I hope you enjoyed reading it as much as I loved writing these stories.

Unable to leave the Purgatory Club behind, I've moved on to the spinoff series, Purgatory Masters. These are full length novels that explore the characters involved in the creation of the Purgatory Club.

Continue reading for an exciting sneak peek into the first in a brand new Purgatory book!

Purgatory Masters: Tucker's Fall

Scandalized professor Maggie Cisco returns to her hometown to lick her wounds and reconsider her future. Her years of personal and professional research into the BDSM lifestyle has landed her in jail, in divorce court and now in the headlines of more newspapers than she cares to count. The worst of all? The entire debacle is being blamed on a bestselling book she hasn't even read!

Just when she thinks her only solution is a tell all memoir, a snowstorm puts her in the path of stunningly handsome, insanely rich and equally intense, Tucker Lewis.

Tucker remembers Maggie well. They once shared a mind-numbing kiss at the annual St. Mary's carnival when her boyfriend wasn't looking. No stranger to scandal, he looks past public opinion to the submissive craving a master's touch and decides then and there what he wants. He's going after Maggie and her heart's kinkiest desires.

Unfortunately, no amount of money can change the sins of the past and when they're certain they know everything there is to know about each other, one discovers a secret they aren't prepared for.

Excerpt:

Tucker Lewis stared into the crowd and wondered when it would all end. He tightened his grip on the shot of Jameson and brought the glass to his lips. Across the bar and generous play space, fake smoke, dancers in chains, and throngs of half-naked partiers filled the club. The intense edge of the Lords of Acid music and the occasional scream of a submissive from the far side of the room fit right in with his dark mood. For better or worse this was the place he'd needed to be tonight.

The Purgatory club had come to be in a different life for him and the longer he sat here watching the scene around him; the less he believed he belonged. Of course his self-imposed exile hadn't helped much. He'd been riding high on life on borrowed time and didn't even know it. All it took was a simple house fire to bring his world crashing down.

"Wow, as I live and breath. Is that you, Tuck?"

Yanked from his mournful thoughts, Tucker focused on the man standing in front of him. Tall and imposing, he wore black leather that emphasized a gleaming baldhead that drew women of all ages. It didn't surprise him that his old friend from better days and one of the best damn rope riggers on the planet stood there with a smug grin.

"Fuck you, Leo."

"C'mon, Tucker. You know I'm not your type. But maybe this one is." Leo tugged on a leash he'd been holding and a very pretty redhead cautiously stepped out from behind him. Even with her eyes cast down, it didn't take much for Tucker to recognize her nervousness. Her hands intertwined with each other repeatedly as she shifted her weight from foot to foot.

Long, red hair brushed the tops of ample breasts that were barely hidden by a thin, black nightie that stopped before her thighs began. But it was the thick leather collar at her neck, branded with two names that stood out to him.

"I see things have changed for you since I last visited."

"Tends to happen when you disappear from the face of the Earth." Leo clapped his shoulder and took a seat on the bench next to him and his lovely submissive went to her knees on the floor at Leo's feet.

Tucker tried to ignore the slight pang inside him. It had been a long time since a submissive had caught his eye but that didn't mean the desire to have one of his own had completely disappeared.

"Will you introduce me to your lovely?"

Leo beamed. "Katie, say hello to Master Tucker. He's an old friend of mine."

With what looked like some reluctance, the little subbie lifted her head and met his gaze. "Hello, Master Tucker. It is nice to meet you."

Immediately her eyes lowered back to the floor.

"You'll have to excuse Katie this evening. She's had a tough time with her commitments lately so Quinn and I have decided to devote this entire week to her correction." Leo stroked his pet's hair and brushed her cheek when she turned toward him.

The pang inside him clamored louder. The affection between Master and submissive was so obvious it was difficult for Tucker not to experience some degree of jealousy, although settling down had never been in his previous plans. "No need to excuse her. I completely understand." Maybe it was time to get back into the scene. He could meet a willing submissive here at the club and work out some of the kinks that had plagued his art this week.

"You thinking about rejoining us? Maybe some play tonight?"

Tucker shrugged, amazed Leo had read his mind. Tucker's body warred with his mind for control. Part of him definitely needed to move on, but the other—well, he wasn't so sure.

"I'd be happy to offer Katie for service tonight. I think it would do her some good. She needs to get her head in the right place for everything she will be put through this week. What do you say?"

Tucker considered the offer while staring at the top of the pretty sub's head. She'd not uttered a word or made a move except for the tiny shudder he'd detected along her shoulder line when Leo offered her services. She impressed him and that wasn't an easy thing to do these days.

He stood from his seat and positioned himself legs apart in front of Katie. Leaning down he cupped her chin and titled her head back until her gaze met his. "I have a feeling I would enjoy your service very much."

She swallowed before a small smile tilted her lips. Whatever trouble she'd been having it was obvious how much she needed whatever Leo wanted to give her.

"It would be my pleasure, Sir."

A part of him really wanted to enjoy Katie. To take part in her discipline and let go of some of the stress he'd endured lately. His self-imposed exile needed to come to an end. He wasn't his father's son anymore. Unfortunately, his body had a mind of its own and wouldn't cooperate like he wanted it to. Flashes of another lovely lady filled his head. A woman he'd not actually laid eyes on in over fifteen years. Maggie Cisco. Professor. Newly single. Closeted submissive.

While he couldn't actually confirm the submissive part yet, his gut told him the truth. She'd been studying BDSM for so long there was no doubt in his mind there was a hidden ache behind her research. And he refused to entertain the alternative of her being a top. That didn't match the Maggie he knew from high school at all. Sure, people changed. He certainly had, but the fundamental core of who you are and what you need on a cellular level doesn't change in adulthood.

He'd bet every last dollar that Maggie possessed the heart of a true submissive, longing to take her place at her Master's side and he'd waited her out long enough. Her reappearance eight weeks ago had sparked more than gossip. Something inside him akin to hunger had unfurled and dug in with razor sharp claws and refused to let go. His recovery had taken a very long time. Too long. Now he needed to rejoin the world, engage in a healthy if somewhat temporary relationship and he'd chosen Maggie to do it with. She didn't know it yet, but he was coming for her.

Tucker's Fall is AVAILABLE NOW at your favorite online retailer.